FINDING BRYCE

THE GREEN BROTHERHOOD: SEAL TEAM XII
BOOK 1

DEBRA PARMLEY

For my readers, with infinite love and gratitude.

1

Virginia Beach

"See you guys at Chicks?" Matthew Hunt "Matt" had opened the door, leaned in, and addressed Diesel and R.T. as they sat at two tables filling out paperwork.

"It's Kik's birthday," he reminded them.

Chicks Oyster Bar Marina was the favored place for SEAL Team Twelve to hang out when they were free to grab a beer and a bite to eat. Many celebrations through the years had been held there, from birthdays, to bachelor parties, and funeral wakes.

"Yeah," Tanner "Diesel" Taylor replied, then he held up the form he was filling out. "When these are done." He laid the paper down again and looked directly at Matt. "That was a clean op. Seems like there ought to be less paperwork instead of more, since we acquired the package and never had to fire one round."

Matt gave a nod, to acknowledge the comment and then said. "You're close to done. See you there."

A mostly by the book, no nonsense sort of man, dealing with what is, was his way. Matt wasn't likely to engage in any kind of discussion about how things ought to be.

Diesel didn't usually complain about things, but he wasn't in his usual mood today. He filled out one more line and then pushed the form across the table to his buddy, Reed "Railroad" Tindall. "We ought to be out running maneuvers, not stuck here in the office doing paperwork."

Reed hated that nickname and was stuck with it, but Diesel had his own nickname for his buddy, and called him R.T. 'Short for railroad tracks' is what he said if anyone asked.

Tanner didn't mind his nickname one bit. Tanner "Diesel" Taylor earned his nickname the first week of basic, when he showed up with grease stains under his fingernails.

Working at his dad's repair shop every week during high school, he'd despaired of his hands, and how the pretty girls would turn him down for dates, thinking his hands were dirty. They didn't know a mechanic could scrub and scrub his hands, and still have stains.

Although it didn't take long for his Navy and SEAL training to wash away those stains, the nickname stuck, along with his ability to repair just about any kind of engine, even in the dark.

In his mind, it was just another skill, but as he'd only followed in his father's footsteps for one year after high school, he was as proud of carrying on his father's legacy into the armed force, as he was of carrying the name.

All the men in his father's side of the family had been mechanics, and his grandfather, and great grandfather had served in the Army during World Wars I and II, which was where they'd learned the ability to work on engines in the dark.

It wasn't that he hadn't wanted to follow in their footsteps even down to their military service, it was that he'd wanted to do more.

Serving as a SEAL was more. Much more.

And he loved every minute of it.

After SEAL training, Diesel never had trouble getting dates again. He was now a lady magnet. Just one of the things his latest girlfriend had more than a little trouble with.

Last night, Kari had broken up with him again, which meant he was free to see whoever he wanted to see.

Diesel watched as R.T. pulled that damn letter out of his pocket again, and with a sad expression, prepared to read the letter again.

"Hey man, you're not going to read that letter again, are you?" Diesel could've repeated most of the letter, having heard it often enough.

"I just don't understand why Becky called it off. She never explained, and she won't answer my phone calls." R.T. bent his head to the letter.

Damn. Dear John letters ought to be written in disappearing ink, or on exploding paper.

Diesel kept his thoughts to himself, but shook his head. Watching R.T, he got an idea.

"Hey. Saturday night. Got plans?"

"Nope." R.T, kept reading." Got laundry."

"You've got plans now." Diesel said. "You can do laundry some other time."

R.T. raised his head, and looked at Diesel.

Good. I got his attention away from that letter.

"Picture lots of chicks in skimpy Halloween costumes," Diesel said.

R.T. groaned. "Costumes?"

"Yeah. Costumes. Don't worry. This will be fun. Costume party is a masquerade."

"I don't have a costume, and there's not enough time to put one together."

"Got you covered. I know a place that rents them, and they're open tonight."

"I don't know, man. I ought to try calling Becky again."

"Come on. This party is a much better time than doing laundry, and crying into your beer. Gonna be plenty of ladies at this party. You know how chicks dig costumes."

"Yeah." R.T. had to admit they did. "Thanks Diesel."

Diesel nodded. "Welcome."

R.T. put the letter away, before picking up the pen again, to finish his task.

It didn't take them long to finish. Then they went home to change clothes, with a plan to meet up at the bar.

After they'd arrived at Chicks, before the other guys arrived, they went to sit out on the deck, and startled a seagull who'd perched on the railing hoping to find food.

The seagull was often there, in that spot. So often, that tourists coming to the marina had started feeding it. Now it came every night, expecting to find food.

The waitress who appeared soon after, to take their orders, had named the bird Fred. She claimed "Fred just wants to be fed."

"What'll you have, guys?" Sheri asked, with a wide smile, between two dimples.

The little waitress was an adorable bundle of energy, and currently dating an airline pilot, who was gone not quite as often as a SEAL would be.

"When are you going to trade that boyfriend in, for a real SEAL?" Diesel teased, already knowing what her answer would be.

"You guys are gone too often, and too long," she said, with a shake of her head, and a laugh.

All the guys teased her this way, and Diesel knew she liked it, though her answer was always the same.

Diesel thought her answer was a lot of hooey. Commercial pilots were gone a lot too, and a woman who could handle that, could handle dating a SEAL.

Women who couldn't, likely wouldn't be able to handle their man being on the road, for any job.

Some women needed more maintenance, just like some cars.

Kari was one of those women. But he and Kari were through.

Diesel enjoyed watching the boats dock at the Marina, which took his mind off Kari just like knocking back a few beers with the guys would take R.T.'s mind off that damn letter.

Cutter, and Matt joined them, and took seats.

"I'll buy a round," "Cutter" Antonius (Tony) Cuttino said.

"What are we celebrating?" R.T. asked.

"My winning at the casino last weekend," Cutter said.

"You have Italian connections?" Sheri asked with a giggle.

The guys knew Cutter had cousins with connections to a casino in New Jersey. When he went home to visit his grandmother, he'd visit the casino and come back with his wins.

"Did you bring me back any cannoli?" Sheri asked.

Last time he'd brought back cannoli his grandma had made.

"Not this time," he said. "Next time, cannoli for you, sweet." He gave her a wink.

She blushed and smiled.

The men placed their beer orders, and she hurried to the bar for their drinks.

"Any of you guys going to the costume party Saturday?" Diesel asked.

"Yeah," Matt said. "I'm gonna go as an IRS auditor."

"Really, man?" R.T. said. "What kind of costume is that?"

"An easy one. Just wear a suit and tie, and carry a calculator," Matt shrugged. "I even got business cards made up to hand out." He reached into his pocket, pulled one out, and handed it to R.T. "I'm here to audit your tax records," he said.

R.T. took the card, and glanced down at it. "That would scare the hell out of a lot of people," he said.

"You are so weird," Diesel shook his head.

"It's simple, cheap, and easy, and I'll have fun with it," Matt said with a shrug.

"That's what costume parties are for," Diesel nodded. "Having fun."

Just after Sheri delivered the beers, Rich, Osprey, and Enrique "Kik" Garcia joined them on the deck, and more beers were ordered.

"Add on some onion rings," Diesel said.

Sheri nodded, and headed for the kitchen.

"You going to the costume party, Rich?" Diesel asked.

"Nah. Costume parties aren't my thing," Richard "Rich" Irvine said.

One of the oldest members of the group, he'd turned down most invites to socialize, since getting back in touch with an old girlfriend from high school at his high school reunion. Now he spent most of his free time with her, trying to get out of the friend zone. She was hesitant about dating a SEAL.

All but Rich would attend the costume party.

Osprey was going as Robin Hood, and would carry a primitive bow he hunted with for fun, and Kik was going as Superman.

"Superman?" R.T. said. "I would've thought you'd want to go as Zorro, or something like that."

"Why, because I'm Latino?" Kik shook his head. He

smoothed his hair back with one hand, and then, reaching for a small section of his bangs, pulled it down, and made it curl. "I got the perfect hair. See? Superman."

All the guys laughed.

"Yeah, man," R.T. said. "I see it."

More SEAL brothers came in the door, which more than doubled the size of their gathering. The entire group was at Chicks tonight. All twenty SEALs.

Diesel glanced around the room. These twenty men were his brothers, and any one of them would have laid down his life for the other.

The Green Brotherhood was like no other, and he took a moment to take the sight of all his brothers in, creating a memory to savor in years to come.

The noise level in the bar rose, but the SEALs weren't the ones shouting and being rowdy.

They kept to themselves, and women in the bar were drawn to the strong silent warriors, like moths to flame. There was clearly something different about these men, the way they carried themselves, and the way they communicated amongst each other, often nonverbally, which set them apart. They exuded a quiet confidence, and their eyes were always taking in their surroundings with a quiet intelligence.

Craig McDonald "Big Mac" showed his Scots Irish heritage, by the multitude of freckles across his nose and cheeks, despite his deeply tanned face. It hid his ruddy complexion, and helped him blend in on their missions. Jet-black hair from his Irish mother saved him from having his fathers red hair, and allowed him to be picked for this special team.

To be on Team Twelve, you had to have dark hair as the team was often sent to South America, and needed to blend in. Blondes and redheads would stand out too much to be included. As a result, the men on Team Twelve could all be described as tall, dark, and handsome.

Blending in, in South America, was something Team Twelve did quite well.

Martin Lopez, the second Hispanic American on the team, was fluent in three languages, English, Spanish, and Portuguese. He was their go to man when it came to native dialects.

Chris Fenner "Fen" had almost gone to college on a chemistry scholarship, but he'd also wanted to become a SEAL. He was their best man with explosives, and a bit of a MacGyver, given his aptitude in chemistry.

He often said it was as much knowing what not to put together with another thing, as it was what to put together. He was also a pretty good cook, which he claimed also had to do with chemistry.

Daniel "Tractor" Edwards grew up on a hay farm, and would have been a fourth-generation farmer, if he'd stayed home on the farm instead of joining the SEALs.

His father had a John Deere collection that men traveled miles to see. Daniel had made the mistake of talking about it too often, early in his training, was handed the nickname "Tractor" and it stuck.

His best buddy in training told him it could've been worse; they could've saddled him with "Farm-boy."

Adam "DaVinci" Burgess was always drawing and doodling, with a pen, or pencil. Tonight, he was already drawing on his cocktail napkin before he'd finished his first beer.

It would have been easy to sit and watch him, instead of focusing on the hot young woman standing nearby, hoping for attention.

Thomas (Tom) Campbell "Soupman" got his nickname after explaining the way to spell his last name, was "Like the soup, man." Once the nickname stuck it was stuck good.

Scott Roberts, "Casper" was like a ghost. He could enter a room and then leave it, without anyone knowing he'd been there.

James Slater "Slim Jim" was a skinny man with toned muscles. His metabolism was so high, he could eat anything and not gain one pound of weight.

Sawyer "Pipes" Ferguson played the bagpipes with the local Scottish group, and sometimes wore a kilt, if performing with the group for weddings or funeral services.

Sam Valente, an Italian American known as "Sammie the Conductor" because of the expressive way he used his hands when he talked, was gesturing animatedly tonight, something he did when he'd drank enough beer.

Peter "Buzz" Horne had a weird snore that sounded like a low buzz.

Jocko "Numbers" Lewis was so good with numbers, they didn't need a calculator when he was around.

And Jake Summers "Oscar" could act any part, and make it believable.

But really, all these men were actors capable of blending in, making anyone believe they were who they pretended to be, and doing what it took to complete a mission.

They were a special team of Navy SEALs, one that few outside the SEAL Teams had ever heard of.

Tonight, they were all at the bar, because it was the rotation of their cycle to have them back in Virginia, before they cycled out again into the next phase. And it just happened to be Kik's birthday.

The beer was flowing, the noise level was rising, and if the good time Kik seemed to be having was any indication, he was going to have a huge hangover tomorrow.

Ordinarily, had he been back home with his family,

there would have been a large family party, with a barbecued goat, music, and beer. After he joined the SEAL team, he'd continued to invite every one of his brothers to celebrate his birthday, and if they were available, they would join in.

Kik was having the time of his life tonight.

All the men trained hard, worked hard, and partied hard.

By the end of the evening, they made sure Kik made it home safe, as he was in no shape to drive, and the bar emptied out, the only occupant left on the patio, a lone seagull with the nickname of Fred, who had returned, hoping for leftovers to eat.

"Come on Pippa, this is the best party of the year, and everyone will be in costume," Cheryl said. "No one will know who you are. It's the perfect chance."

It was only the tenth time Cheryl had asked her to go to the Halloween party.

Finally, tired of being bugged about it, Pippa said, "Okay, I'll go."

"Great!" Cheryl's eyes widened, and she grabbed both of Pippa's hands, squeezing tight as she bounced on her heels. "You're going to be so glad you changed your mind. We're going to have a blast."

For once, Pippa would take a page from her mother's diary, and live in the moment.

As her mother had said, "Joyce, my dear, you haven't yet learned that life must be grasped in the moment."

Joyce Pippalousa Smith never gave out her birth name. Her full middle name had always been an embarrassment to her, though she did like her daddy's nickname for her.

He was the only one to call her "Pippa", and she missed him dearly. Her mother had always called her Joyce.

After her mother had made her announcement, she'd gone sailing off to Hawaii with a new man, who kept a boat at his summer home. "Waiting just gives you more likelihood you'll miss out. Your father may be dead, but I'm not."

Her mother was the kind of woman who couldn't stand to be alone, and one of her friends had been waiting in the wings, ready to date her.

Thinking back to the huge blow-up Pippa and her younger sister, Jeanie Magic Smith, had with their mother the day before their mother left town, made Pippa wonder where her mother was now, and reminded her, she needed to call Jeanie this weekend, and get caught up.

Mother could be anywhere. I have no idea how to reach her at sea. I don't even have her new number.

But as Jeanie often said, 'The phone works both ways.' And her sister's number hadn't changed.

Though usually Pippa was the one who had to call her sister. Months could go by, if she didn't, before Jeanie got around to calling her.

For once, Pippa was going to take a page from her mother's book. She was going to live a little.

It had been a long time since she'd gone out and had fun, and she'd always loved costume parties and Halloween.

"Now, what are you gonna be?" Cheryl asked.

"I don't know. I haven't had time to think about it," Pippa said, her tone wry. She'd only agreed a second ago.

Cheryl waved a hand, and continued in her rapid-fire way; clearly thrilled Pippa was going. "We can go to the costume shop after we get off work."

"Okay," Pippa said.

A masquerade party seemed safe enough. It was unlikely that her ex would be there. She'd moved several states away from Stan Nitty, and hoped to never see him again.

❧

After work, they headed to That Magical Place, a store which sold costumes, and decorations for Halloween.

"Do you have any sexy costumes for women?" Cheryl asked.

The clerk grinned. "Yes, we do. Follow me, and I'll show you. Do you have any themes in mind?"

"I looked up your selections online. I think I'd like to be a woodland fairy," Pippa said. "With wings, and pointed ears, and everything." Now that she was getting excited about going, why not go full-on fantasy?

"Oh, fun," Cheryl said. "I'm going as a sexy nurse. Maybe I can play nurse with one of those hot Navy SEALs tomorrow night. Is your costume going to be sexy?"

"Well..." Pippa considered the costume she remembered from the website. "It's short and shows a lot of leg, and a lot of cleavage. It's also cheap, which I need. I don't have much budget for a costume."

"Want me to help you with your makeup and hair?"

"Oh, would you? That would be awesome." Pippa knew Cheryl was good at doing hair and makeup.

"Yeah, I'll come over an hour before and help you get ready," Cheryl said.

"Thanks, Cheryl." As she did every day, Pippa thanked her instincts for bringing her here to Virginia. Her sister had been only too willing to give her safe harbor when she'd needed it, and she lived just an hour away.

"No problem, Miss Pipp."

Pippa wrinkled her nose. "You're not gonna call me that at the party, I hope."

12

"No, I'm not gonna call you at all, 'til we agree it's time to go home. We're gonna circulate as single ladies, so the men will be more likely to approach us," Cheryl winked.

"Oh, right," Pippa nodded. "Good thinking."

The next day, Pippa's cousin Louise called her at work and left a message for her to call back. Far from being a normal call, Louise would only have called if someone had died or something very big had happened. So as Pippa called Louise back, she held her breath. "Hey, Louise. What's happened?"

"This time it's good news, Pippa," Louise said. "You won't have to worry about Stan anymore. He's been sent to prison for three years. Felonious assault. He beat up a guy in a bar. That was bad enough. But then he went back and beat him some more. The guy was hurt bad, and they had to call an ambulance. Stan claimed it wasn't his fault, and the other guy did this and did that, but everything was caught on the bar's security cameras. And it didn't hurt that they had pictures of the bruises he left on your neck, or that you have a restraining order out on him, already on record. He's obviously a violent and dangerous man. I'm so glad he's been sent to prison and won't be out for a long time. I couldn't wait to tell you."

Pippa breathed a sigh of relief. Stress began to drain out of her body. "Oh, that is good news. He can't find me now, and suddenly show up on my doorstep to hurt me. Not while he's in prison. So, I'm safe. Finally. No more looking over my shoulder, worrying he might be the man in the baseball cap behind me. I'm safe, finally safe!"

She felt like dancing and spinning around the room.

"Yes, you are," Louise said. "Does this mean you'll come home, now?"

"I am home," Pippa said. "Virginia is my home now, and I just started taking a couple college classes."

"So, you're staying?"

"Yes." Pippa didn't say that she never wanted to move back to her hometown, but she surely felt that way. She'd escaped a horrible marriage, a depressing house, and a town, which lost more jobs every year, and she never wanted to go back.

There was no future there. Only the past. And the past was over and done. Finally.

"Well, all right. If that's what you want," Louise said. "I just want you to be happy."

"Oh, I am happy," Pippa said. "Happier than I've been in a very long time."

The night of the party, Pippa let Cheryl into her apartment, and they went straight into her bathroom, where she had a curling iron already plugged in. She wanted to look different tonight, and her long brown hair usually hung straight. Most days, she loved a wash-and-go kind of lifestyle and rarely wore makeup. But tonight, she wanted a little glamour—her hair curling, smoky-sparkling makeup, and fairy ears glued onto her ears.

Cheryl curled Pippa's hair until it had ringlets at the ends, which gave it a whole lot more body. Once she finished applying makeup to Pippa's face, Cheryl took gold glitter and sprinkled it in Pippa's hair and across her bared shoulders. Spaghetti straps held the silky fairy dress up, leaving a lot of skin bare. The way the dress was cut in back, there was no way to wear a bra with this one.

It was the most daring thing Pippa had ever worn in public.

"Might as well use it up," said Cheryl before sprinkling the rest of the vial of glitter down Pippa's cleavage.

Pippa felt the glitter whisper between her breasts. "Cheryl!" she said, laughing. "I don't need it everywhere."

"Oh, but I think you do," Cheryl said. "Keep him looking for the end of that glitter trail, and you'll have his attention for sure. Then he'll be hard at attention, and you'll have some real fun."

Pippa kept chuckling. "I'll bedazzle him with my cleavage."

"You know it." Cheryl winked and tossed the empty container into the trashcan. "Ready to go?"

"Yes, I just need my tiny purse."

"Here." Cheryl reached into her purse for two condoms and handed them to Pippa. "Be prepared, because those Navy boys are not always like boy scouts, and some of them really get around."

"Oh, right." They hadn't talked much about Pippa's former life, only that she'd divorced a man who was no good and that she was trying to make a new life without complications. She hadn't hinted at her ex's violent tendencies.

Cheryl, being a party girl, understood the "no complications" bit. She never dated a guy longer than six months. Said it got claustrophobic if they lingered any longer.

"Thanks. I hadn't thought to pick those up," Pippa said.

"Always keep one in your purse and some in your nightstand. Tonight's a chance for you to have fun without the hassle of a date. But if you need more than two of these, you're on your own, girlfriend."

Unable to stop a blush, Pippa shook her head. "I won't need more than two."

I'll be lucky to need one, she thought. It had been over a year since she'd had sex, and she missed it. In the good times, at the beginning of her marriage, before everything went terribly bad, sex had been good, with that rush of attraction that went straight to her core, lighting everything up, just like fairy lights. It had been magic.

I want that again, even if for just one night. This is a start. And no one will even know who I am. This is perfect.

2

Pippa watched the redheaded bartender as he mixed drinks and wondered what he was making. "Those look good," she said, pointing toward the colorful drinks. "What are they?"

"Hurricanes," he said, smiling.

"I can't believe you've never had a hurricane," Cheryl said. "They are so, so good. You should try one."

Pippa told the bartender, "I'll try a hurricane, please."

"Coming right up," he said and handed her a glass with a pineapple slice on the rim and a drink umbrella on it. "Enjoy your first hurricane."

She took a sip. "Ooh, these are good," she said. The drink was fruity and cold. It went down easily. "I think I'll stick with these tonight."

"Good choice," Cheryl said, eying a tall man across the room. "Have fun, Pipp. I'm off to try my luck."

"Good luck," she said, taking another sip and scanning the crowd. The house was packed with guests, everyone wearing masks. She loved the riot of color and the mysteriousness of the masks. She stood sipping and watching the crowd for a few moments, lost in thought.

She mused it was going to be hard to decide which guy

to try to approach. There were a lot of handsome, fit guys. But that's what Cheryl had predicted, living so near to a place where SEALs trained.

Her drink was half gone by the time she gathered the nerve to move. Crossing the room by weaving in and out of the crowd, she headed for a dark-haired pirate. She planned to ask him if he knew the way to the pirate treasure, but then he moved toward a woman and kissed her on the cheek.

Oh, too late, she thought. *I need to be faster. And maybe not pick a guy clear across the room.* She continued the internal pep talk, trying to work up her courage to ask one of the guys to dance.

She circulated, and soon, her drink was empty. She headed back to the bartender for a refill. The hurricanes were good, and the warmth of the room from all the people was making her thirsty.

Holding her now full glass, she decided to step outside onto the covered back porch and get some cooler air. The stars were out, and the night sky would be pretty.

She stood outside long enough to finish her drink as she counted the stars and listened to the people around her talking. As she turned to go back inside, to get another drink, she stumbled a little on the doormat.

She'd gotten tipsier than she'd expected. The hurricanes had snuck up on her. She couldn't remember the last time she'd allowed herself to relax at all, let alone drink.

And then he was there, coming through the front door, just as she stumbled and looked up. He was like a Greek God, with his tanned chest and washboard abs that made her want to run her fingers up and down them. And he moved with such smooth and controlled command. But no, as he got closer, she saw she'd mistaken his costume.

Instead of a Greek God, he was wearing a gladiator's outfit with a black mask.

For everyone who came to the front door without a mask, a black mask was handed to them before they were allowed inside. No mask, no entry. So, everyone who'd come without a mask was wearing the same black type of mask. Like he was. And the room was full of men wearing black masks. Yet in a room full of men wearing black masks, he stood out. Something about the way he stood, taking in the room, something about the way he moved made him stand out.

He spoke to the cowboy who'd entered with him and then they broke away from each other. He moved through the crowd and stopped halfway across the room to talk to a tall, thin man who wore a jester's costume. They both laughed about something.

She watched the gladiator's perfect white teeth flash beneath the mask, which contrasted with his tan. With an unobstructed view, still, she knew he was a good-looking man. Sipping her drink, she continued to watch him. She had yet to talk to anyone. Her shyness had gotten in the way, or her timing was always off when she made the attempt. But after finishing off that second drink, she felt much bolder.

Curious now, she thought to get close enough to hear his voice. Already she felt drawn to him, but she needed to hear his voice. She couldn't have explained why. It shouldn't have made any difference if they were only going to get together once, this night, then never see each other again. But it did matter.

As she neared, she heard him speak, his voice low, deep, and strong. Goose bumps prickled on her skin. She moved nearer.

He was talking about ghost tours with the other man and two women.

"I'd go for the historical aspect," he said. "I don't expect anyone would really see a ghost with that many people tramping through a room, and most people don't know how to be quiet." He laughed. "They'd scare the mice away."

"Not all of us have the training at being stealthy, like you SEALs," a woman wearing a saloon dancer's outfit said. Bursting out of the top half of her costume, her cleavage was getting plenty of attention from the men around her. "But you can sneak up on me any time."

"I'm not in the habit of sneaking up on women," he said. "Not my style."

What was his style? Pippa wondered. *Whatever it is, I'm sure I'd like it.*

His voice was doing funny things to her insides.

Listening to him is so nice I'd enjoy hearing him read the side of a cereal box.

When a large man nearly stepped on her foot, she moved backward and glanced up the next instant to find the gladiator was gone, heading to the dance floor with one of the women.

I'm just not having any luck, Pippa thought. Sighing, she headed to the bar for a third hurricane. *I must get better at this. Courage. I can do this. I will just go up to him and say...* Her thoughts froze.

The bartender handed her a refreshed drink.

She took a sip, her thoughts a jumble as she tried to think of what to do next.

I know what I'll do. I'll ask him to dance. Since he's dancing now, he obviously dances. I just must get back over there before he dances with someone else. Oh, how do men do this? The asking. It's much harder than I thought.

She made her way back to where he was dancing and

hovered beside a potted palm. The moment he'd finished, and the two moved apart, she went up to him, even though her stomach had started doing flips.

Taking her courage in both hands, she gave him a smile. "Hello," she said. "Would you like to dance with me?

Now that's what I like, Diesel thought as he looked down at the brown-haired woman with green eyes, wearing some kind of fairy costume. The glitter in her hair, across her shoulders, and down her cleavage, along with her question, made him want to smile.

A woman who knows what she wants and asks for it. Direct, and to the point. I like that.

"I would be honored," he said and held out his hand. He noted that if she moved closer, he'd see more of the glitter spilling down the inside her dress.

Diesel was six-feet-two, and this delightful creature couldn't have been more than five-five.

She moved closer to him and placed her soft hand in his.

Yes. A very good view.

He pulled her close, and they moved to the music. "May I have your name?"

"I am the fairy of the green wood," she said. "I'm a woodland fairy, and I love nothing better than... wood."

He chuckled. *There are so many things I might say in response. Did she know the direction this conversation might take?* She'd said wood, not "the woods."

Testing her, he said, "Tell me more... about how you love... wood."

Her chest quivered with soft laughter. "I love wood so much I can't help but touch it," she said. "It's hard to keep my hands off rough bark."

The little green-eyed minx. How far would she take this? "Interesting," he said. "What do you do when you touch it?"

She swallowed, and then drew a deep breath that

caused the sparkles on her chest to shimmer. "Well, I run my hand up and down it," she said, sounding a little breathless. "I like to feel how hard it is, how strong and durable."

He pulled her close to him so she could feel his muscles beneath his gladiator costume.

Her eyes widened. "Mm," she said. "I like touching you."

He bent and whispered in her ear. "Something needs to be done. If I step away…"

"Don't step away," she said, her smile turning seductive. "Dance me out of this room and into another."

"As you command, fae enchantress."

He moved them through the main room and into the hallway. Then, away from the others, he tipped up her chin and said, in a low voice. "Tell me what you want."

Her lips pressed together then stretched into a slow whimsical grin. "I want to touch your bare skin," she said. "To feel your hard muscles, all over."

Her words were the sexiest he'd ever heard in his life. Truly, she was an enchantress, and he was about to have great sex here tonight. With an over-the-top flourish, he bowed. "You have but to ask," he said. "My wood is yours to command."

Giggling, a sound, which made her seem more adorable than seductress, made him laugh out loud.

She took him by the hand and led him down the hall. "I don't know this house or where to go," she said, and for the first time her voice sounded less than confident.

"Allow me." He pushed on one door, which was locked. "Come," he said. "We'll find a place." The third door he tried was unlocked, and the room was empty. He pulled her inside quick before anyone saw them and then closed and locked the door.

She looked up at him with wide green eyes beneath the

mask, and he thought for the first time that perhaps she was in over her head as he saw uncertainty.

Diesel didn't do uncertainty when it came to women and sex.

"Let's establish something here, before we return to the fantasy and play time," he said. "You want to have sex, yes?"

"Yes." She breathed the word out as if she were relieved.

Okay, so she's playing out her fantasy right now, but she did look as though she'd never done this before. As if she were unsure.

"I have protection," she said and reached for her bag.

She is an adorable creature, he thought. The mix of assertive seductress and shy, uncertain woman was fascinating. Her green eyes fascinated him; with their myriad of shades and emotions he'd seen since she'd said "hello".

He reached for the hem of his costume, pulled it up, and then tucked it into the belted waistband.

"Look what you've done to me with your fairy magic," he whispered, watching her eyes as they looked down and widened.

She looked up at him again and gave a quick nod.

Then she noticed the long white scar that ran down his right arm and ran her forefinger down the scar. Again, she looked up at him with those green take me now eyes peering out of her mask. "What is this from?" she asked.

"Long time ago. I was working in my dad's shop and a hot muffler fell on it."

"Oh, that had to hurt," she said.

"It did," he said. "But chicks dig scars." He winked at her. Then he took her by the hand.

He reached for and pulled the top of her fairy costume down, to bare her breasts and glitter spilled out everywhere.

"Magic fairy dust." He laughed. "I'd kiss them, but they're covered in glitter." He brushed at the glitter covering them, a light touch.

Her breath was changing, as were her eyes, the hazel green changing to more of a deeper green.

He let her go. "Lie down," he said.

She backed onto the bed.

He bent, hovered over her, watching her through his mask, watching as her eyes changed through each moment as he touched her, moving her closer to be ready to join with him. The masks forced them to focus on each other with an intensity neither had experienced before when making love.

Neither broke eye contact and they wordlessly connected, the masks giving the dream like quality to it all.

When she found her release, in her eyes he felt he'd glimpsed something rare, something he'd like to see again.

Pippa exhaled, spent. When she took her next breath, his scent lingered, making her want to snuggle next to him. Dancing close, touching his warm bare skin, and inhaling his scent had nearly done her in—before they'd even begun to remove clothing.

The chemistry between them was incredible.

When he spoke, his voice reached something deep inside her. From the start, she'd been a goner. That voice, combined with the gentle but intense passion of his love-making, was beyond anything she could've imagined.

If there is magic in the world, this is it.

Her thoughts drifted into that magic place, and her eyelids drifted downward.

Afterward, they lay together without speaking, sharing those final moments.

She didn't know what to say. This was beyond what she'd expected. This was deeper. Not a quickie. Their joining felt almost... sacred.

His hand reached for her mask before he bent to kiss her.

Her heart tripped. She stopped his hand with hers. "We

won't unmask," she said. "I want to remember us, just like this."

"All right," he said. "May I have your name now?"

Although it nearly killed her, she remembered why she'd wanted to keep this anonymous. This night had been magical, but she couldn't take the risk.

"Woodland fairy," she said, her voice firmer now. "And you are my gladiator."

He pulled away and clasped his fist to his chest. "I am your gladiator."

"Thank you for this," she said. "My fantasies came true."

"No, my enchantress," he replied. "Thank *you*."

They exchanged smiles.

She adjusted her fairy costume.

He dangled her panties from his finger, holding them out to her, teasing.

Feeling reckless, she tossed back her hair. "I can go without."

The thought made him groan. "Careful. Unless you want a repeat."

She wrinkled her nose at the panties. "They aren't very comfortable."

"Then don't wear them. Be comfortable. But also, be safe." He held out his hand. "Will you let me give you a ride home, to make sure you arrive safe?"

She shook her head. "I came with a co-worker. I'll ride home with her."

So much for figuring out where she lived. But she'd set the rules. He'd respect them. "I'll escort you back to the party."

Her hand was already on the door. "I'm good. No need to."

As he watched her go, he couldn't help disagreeing. There was *every* need to go with her.

Protective was his nature. But he was also good at surveillance. He'd watch until the women were safe in their car and heading home. She'd never know.

The moment he got in his car to follow her and removed his cell phone from the glove box he saw that Kira had been blowing up his phone with calls and texts. It was like the woman had a sixth sense when he was having a good time with another woman. Since they'd broken up, again, it was none of Kira's business who he was with tonight or what he was doing.

Ignoring the phone, he set it on the passenger seat and proceeded to follow his mystery woman at a distance.

All was going well until a semi-tractor trailer hit something and went sliding across the highway. All traffic behind the semi-tractor stopped.

Diesel stood on the floorboards of his car to see above his car, trying to glimpse past the wreck to the little blue Chevy he'd been following.

No sight of her. She'd driven on.

He didn't have her name or her number so he couldn't even call to make sure she got home safely. That bothered him.

Two days later, he had his duffel packed and was on his way out of the country, still wishing he knew how to contact her. He couldn't get the mystery woman out of his head.

There was just something about her...

I'll look for her when I get back. For now, I must focus on the mission.

～

"**M**aybe I should've given him my number," Pippa said, the corners of her mouth drooping.

Cheryl shrugged. "I think you did it just right. You had a

night of great sex with a hot guy, and no strings or complications, because he has no idea who you are."

She couldn't help feeling wistful. "He seemed very nice, and I don't mean just the hard body and great sex."

Cheryl flicked her fingers. "Focus on that hard body and the great sex and let the rest go."

Still, Pippa couldn't. "I mean, he seemed like the kind of guy you could introduce to your parents and might want to marry. I really liked him," Pippa said. "And there was something magical about our lovemaking."

Cheryl rolled her eyes. "That was the hurricanes talking. And the costumes, and the sleeping-with-a-complete-stranger fantasy. That's not real life, Pippa. You don't need complications right now. Not when you're trying to finish school. Having a man in your life just means having a guy *who wants your attention.* And then, when something goes wrong, and it always does, you'll have the heartbreak and drama of a breakup to deal with. Do you even have time for that?"

Cheryl made complete sense. However, Pippa's heart wouldn't be quiet.

Silly things, hearts. They get us into all sorts of trouble.

"Not really. You're right, I don't have time. And my track record with men isn't good. Getting to know him better might have ruined everything. No guy is that perfect," Pippa said, pouting her lips.

"Exactly. You needed to have sex with someone. You did that, and now you can move on. Think of it as a great night and a great memory and leave it there. No second guessing."

"Yeah, you're right... I guess," Pippa said.

"Now maybe you'll consider dating. Nothing serious, just going out maybe every other weekend. Have some fun. Stop staying in every night."

"No, I can't," Pippa said.

"You weren't afraid to have sex with a stranger. That's living bold, Pippa. But you're afraid to go out on a date. What are you so afraid of?"

Do I dare confide in her? Pippa watched Cheryl, pondering. *She's kept what I told her private so far. Maybe I can. She's the closest thing to a best friend that I have.*

"I was married once."

Cheryl settled back in her seat and looked at Pippa. "I knew there was something. What happened?"

"It was bad," Pippa said. "Not at first, but later. My dad passed six months after I married Stan Nitty and after he passed, the honeymoon period was over. It turned bad fast."

"Having your dad around gave you some protection."

"Yes and no," Pippa said. "Dad was a vocal kind of man, and he didn't put up with injustice, but he was a peace-loving newspaper reporter, who'd never fired a gun. He didn't like the fact Stan was fifteen years older than me, or the way he insisted everyone needed to stock up for doomsday. Stan made his own bullets."

"Wow," Cheryl said. "The two were complete opposites. So, what did you see in Stan?"

"He was charming at first. Always showing up with sweet words, flowers, bears."

"Bears?"

"I collected stuffed teddy bears. When he found out, he brought me one every week. He tried everything to charm me into going out with him and then to keep going out with him. Everything he does is extreme, and he wanted me, so he pursued me like he pursues everything. Full throttle."

"High school boys didn't stand a chance, competing for your attention against a grown man with experience," Cheryl said.

"True. I thought he wanted me more than they did. He said he'd do anything to win me and to make me his."

"So, you got married and things went south fast. What happened? Did he hurt you?"

Pippa nodded. "He's serving time now for felonious assault. Beat up a guy in a bar, but that wasn't good enough for him. He turned around and went back in and beat him again. They got it on tape and put him away."

"Wow. That's more than full throttle," Cheryl said. "He sounds like bad news. Real bad news. No wonder you're such a homebody and never go out."

"I'm not afraid to go out," Pippa said. "I just need to be cautious. Real cautious."

"That's why you never relax," Cheryl nodded. "You're always looking out windows or doors instead of giving your whole attention when someone is talking."

"It's not disinterest," Pippa said. "I'm still listening."

"Yeah, I get that now. I'm glad you told me."

"I am too."

"Is Pippa your real name?"

"Kind of. My parents met at a bluegrass festival and were inseparable from day one. They decided my middle name had to be part of the name of the festival where I was conceived."

"How cool."

"Not really. That's a lot to load onto a child. Brings on teasing, kids picking on you. It made me shy in school. I'd stick my nose in a book and try to pretend no one had just hurt my feelings."

"You found a way to run away to another world," Cheryl said. "In books."

"Yeah," Pippa nodded.

"So, what happened with you and Stan?"

"One New Year's Eve, Stan went out of his mind. He'd been drinking a lot and was very angry. He tried to choke me to death. Wrapped his hands around my neck and squeezed until I passed out. I was still in a daze, grieving my father and wasn't paying enough attention to Stan. He couldn't handle me not always giving him my full attention, so he turned mean."

"And he'd never done anything before that which let you know he might be dangerous?"

"There were signs," Pippa said. "I didn't want to believe he was that bad, that I was with the wrong guy. He tried to make me think the things he did were my fault."

"It was not your fault," Cheryl said.

"I know that now," Pippa said. "The first time Stan put a fist through the wall, I knew I needed a getaway plan."

"So, you made a plan and then when he went crazy you were ready and got out," Cheryl said.

"Not exactly," Pippa shook her head. "I knew I needed one but hadn't made one yet. It was like planning would mean I'd given up hope the marriage could ever be a good one. Sometimes he was nice to me. I was very confused back then and he knew exactly how to play me."

"Well, hell yeah, he had fifteen years of living experience on you to know how to manipulate and get his way," Cheryl said. "You married what, right out of high school?"

"Yeah." Pippa shrugged. "I was young and naïve."

"Virgin too, I bet."

"Oh yes." Pipped nodded. "That was very important to him. He talked about that a lot. Being the first and me being pure."

"Jeeze Louise. No wonder you're not used to going out with guys. He was your only until when?"

Pippa gave a blushing smile. "Until my gladiator."

"If anyone deserved a night of total fantasy fulfillment, it's you. Girlfriend, I don't even know what to say. I'm glad you got away from Stan Nitty and that you're okay now."

"Thanks Cheryl. I'm glad too."

"So, after he choked you, then you had to leave."

Pippa nodded. "The night Stan lost his mind; he tore the bedroom door off the hinges and came after me. I knew then I had to run but then he had his hands around my neck, and I blacked out. The minute I woke up ready to run, I looked for him and he was still drunk and passed out on the living room couch, snoring. I had to get out of there while I still could, so I grabbed my purse and ran out the back door with only my purse and the clothes on my back."

"Damn. That had to be scary. You're a brave woman, Pippa Marks."

"I changed my name to Marks, legally. I got rid of Nitty, and I wanted a new name, one it would be easier to step away from my past with."

The restraining order she had against Stan was in her old name, and she didn't fully trust it to keep him away so there would be no point in getting a new one. That she had one made him very angry. He wasn't going to listen to a piece of paper. She wasn't even sure he'd listen to a policeman or a gun

Stan had always seemed like a force of nature. He was strong and tough minded and loved a challenge.

Likely a new restraining order would only make him come after her. And she was all the way across the country now, where she was much harder to find, and she was using a new name which she didn't want him to know.

"I'm guessing you're not from Virginia," Cheryl said. "You have that midwestern accent."

"I'm from Yellow Springs, Ohio. It's in between Dayton and Springfield Ohio."

"So, you came here and got a job in the grocery," Cheryl smiled. "I'm glad you did, or we wouldn't have met."

"I'm glad too." Pippa smiled.

"Now that I know, I won't keep pushing you to go out

with guys. Maybe what you need is one good guy instead of dating ones who could turn out to be losers."

"Yeah, but I'm in no hurry for that either. I need to finish my classes and get a better job. That, and work is keeping me busy."

Pippa was learning secretarial skills at the local community college and working at the grocery store while hoping her crazy ex would stay in Ohio and not show up in Virginia looking for her.

Though she'd been divorced for over a year, dating was the last thing on her mind. She didn't trust a new date to be the man he claimed to be. Once burned, twice shy. She wasn't sure she'd ever date again.

"I understand," Cheryl said. "Would you be up for a girl's night out every so often?"

"Yes, that sounds like fun."

"Cool beans," Cheryl said. "It will be. And in the meantime, you had a great time at the party, right?"

"I did." Pippa smiled. "It was the best night of my life."

"You'll be having happy dreams of this guy."

"Oh yes, I will." Pippa grinned. "My gladiator."

"You have a glow," Cheryl said.

"Maybe that's because I'm happy." Pippa smiled.

That happiness lasted until the morning sickness started. Starting each day with salty crackers and slow nibbles of an apple slice just to be able to get out of bed without being sick, Pippa knew this was more than a flu.

The at home pregnancy test confirmed it.

She called to make a doctor's appointment and thought, *what am I going to do?*

3

____

This time her mystery man had given her a glow, but it was a glow of pregnancy.

There could be only one father.

A man, with the body of a gladiator; a voice, which reached deep inside of Pippa; and a face, she'd never fully seen.

A man whose name she didn't know.

"But we used a condom," she told her doctor in bewilderment. "How did this happen?"

"Condoms are not one hundred percent protection. There is a small margin of error. Around one percent," the doctor said.

"Great," Pippa said. "And I'm a one-percenter."

He cleared his throat. "Do you want this child?"

She blinked. Everything was happening so fast. She needed to think. But about this, she felt no hesitation.

Her hand moved to her belly, an automatic protective move.

Of course, I want this baby. No matter who his or her daddy is. I'm going to be a mother.

"Yes."

"All right," he said, nodding and pulling out his prescription pad from his pocket. "We need to get you on some good prenatal vitamins and schedule your next visit."

As she left his office, Pippa still couldn't believe it.

I'm going to be a mother. A single mom. This wasn't how I'd thought my life would turn out.

When she'd set out for the Halloween party, planning to have a memorable evening she'd look back on for the rest of her life, she hadn't planned this. Now, she was having trouble wrapping her mind around the consequence.

The next day at work, she told Cheryl and watched Cheryl's jaw drop.

"Oh honey, I'm sorry. I never thought this would happen." Cheryl said.

"I didn't either," Pippa said, giving her friend a tiny smile.

"Girl, you have the worst luck," Cheryl said.

"I'm trying not to think of it that way," Pippa said. "This baby, though not planned, will be loved just as much as any other baby."

Apparently for around one percent of the female population, contraception did not work. The doctor had explained this was true of using the pill, or a condom, or any other form of birth control.

Lucky me, to fall into that one percent.

She thought about looking for the handsome gladiator. But how would she ever find him?

I don't even know his name. And I can hardly walk onto the Naval base and say, hey, one of your SEAL's has knocked me up, can you help me find him. They'd think I was a real slut.

But I don't sleep around. He was the second man I ever slept with. Now, he'll be my last.

My life will be complicated enough with a baby without bringing a man or dating into it.

She bought a book of baby names and poured through the book. For a girl, she picked out the name Tania which meant 'fairy queen.' She only got as far as the B's when looking for a boy's name. Bryce seemed to jump out of the page for her. Bryce meant 'of Britain' which wasn't the reason she picked the name. She couldn't have explained to anyone why she'd picked that one, other than it just felt right.

The day Bryce was born, and she held him for the first time, looking down at his dark hair and his sweet little face, she felt that rush of mother love first time mothers feel and thought, *oh you look like your daddy. I wonder where he is now and what he would think of you if he could see you. I wish I could show you to him.*

A single tear spilled down her cheek amid her happiness and love for her child.

Every child deserved a mother and a father who loved them. She wished she could give that to her new son.

She closed her eyes and sent up a prayer.

Please bring Bryce's father home safely and please, if it is meant to be and best for our child, please bring him to us.

Maybe someday, if her prayer was answered, it would happen.

Two years had passed since Diesel had made love to the beautiful fairy princess with no name. He'd often dreamed of her, but the SEAL missions he was sent on kept him busy on deployments and not back in the states often.

One year had slid into two, until he'd thought of her less and less.

She was now a fond memory and a good dream when she showed up as he slept.

This week, he was back in town, and his father was visiting. It was great seeing his dad and showing him around, introducing him to the guys. His father wasn't getting any younger, and the pride in his eyes said everything to Diesel.

Bryce Taylor was enjoying the visit with his son, but it would soon be at an end.

Diesel had been called in for a meeting and would be shipping out again, soon. Since they couldn't have lunch together today, his dad decided to pick up lunch somewhere and take it to the park to enjoy the great weather. Too soon, he'd have to go back home where the weather wasn't as nice.

Sitting on a park bench, he watched as a little boy about two years of age played in the park.

Something about the boy drew his eye.

As the boy got closer, Bryce blinked twice to clear his eyes, and then rubbed them, but nothing changed, and the sense of *déjà vu* could not be blinked or rubbed away.

The boy playing in the park had dark wavy hair and dark brown eyes. The shape of his brows and the lively dark brown eyes full of mischief reminded him of Tanner, when he was two years old. This little boy was the spitting image of his son.

Bryce could have stepped back in time to be looking at his own son. The boy resembled Tanner so much it was uncanny.

As he spoke, the boy's voice took Bryce back twenty-six years. He even sounded like Tanner.

Good Lord, he could be Tanner's.

His gaze went immediately to the mother. She was young, with long brown hair, and green eyes. She wasn't wearing a ring.

Is she a single mom? Had she dated Tanner?

He had to find out. He didn't want to alarm the woman

or make her think he was some kind of creep, trying to get close to her for nefarious purposes.

How could he ask the questions pressing on him that he wanted to ask?

Bryce watched mother and child walk to the parking lot, holding hands, and then he stood, gathering his half-eaten sandwich. Following them, he dropped the rest of his sandwich into a trashcan he passed on the way, his appetite gone.

Mother and child moved toward an older model blue Chrysler with a red door. It had obviously been in an accident. He hoped neither of them had been hurt.

She opened the car door and put the boy into his car seat. Then she buckled him in and closed the door. Getting into the driver's seat, she closed the door and turned the car ignition over.

Her car wouldn't start.

He could see the frustration on her face.

A grin crossed his face. Someone was looking out for him and for her.

Good thing I'm a mechanic, he thought. *I can fix this and maybe learn more about her and the boy.*

He walked over to their car and said, "Having car trouble? Can I help?"

She scrunched her nose. "It won't start."

"Pop the hood, and I'll take a look at it."

She popped the hood.

He went around to the front of the car, lifted the hood, and looked inside. Then he came back around to the window and said, "I see your problem. Let me show you."

She got out and checked on her child in the back seat in his car seat before walking around to the front of the car with him. The boy was starting to doze off.

"It's getting close to his nap time," she said.

"He's a cute little tyke. What's the boy's name?" Bryce asked.

"His name is Bryce," She smiled.

Bryce froze when he heard the boy's name.

If Tanner was his dad, then the boy's mother had named the boy after his grandfather.

His emotions threatened to overtake him, and rare were the times in his life that this had happened. He blinked away a tear, focusing on the car again, redirecting his mind with a firm control. "Here's your problem," he said. "See all this corrosion on this battery terminal?"

"What's corrosion?" she asked.

"See this salty-looking white stuff?"

"Yes," she said, her tone saying she wished she didn't.

He grabbed the negative terminal, and the loose wire came right off. "It's loose. That's what's causing this." He pulled his Leatherman multi-tool out of his pocket.

"That looks like a big Swiss army knife."

He pulled out the blade and scraped as much of the corrosion off as he could. Then he put the wire back on the terminal and took a pair of pliers and tightened the nut. "Now try it," he said.

She got back in the car and tried the ignition again. It started right up.

He closed the hood with a bang. "You should be good to go now, but you might want to get this checked out by your mechanic. I don't have my other tools with me. It would be a good idea to have a competent mechanic go over this car. Cars this age need good maintenance to keep them running."

She appeared to wince. "Yes, I should probably do that. Thank you. Are you a mechanic? I don't have one."

"Yes, but I live in another state. My son is also a mechanic and a Navy SEAL. If you need some work done,

I'm sure he'd be willing to help you when he's not off on deployment. His name is Tanner. Tanner Taylor."

He watched her face, but not even one iota of change came over her, when she heard his son's name. So, he tried again. "But all his SEAL buddies call him Diesel."

Again, she showed no reaction.

Bryce wasn't sure what to think now. His gut was telling him that the little boy, who was now dozing in his car seat, had to be Tanner's. "I'm Bryce Taylor."

She held out her hand. "I'm Pippa. It's nice to meet you. Thank you again for fixing my car."

"You're welcome," he said. "Well, you'd best be getting the little fella home to sleep in his own bed."

Soon Pippa and little Bryce were on their way home, and Bryce Taylor had the information he'd wanted. She was a single mom. The boy was two. And his name was Bryce.

This irony was unbelievable to Bryce Taylor.

The boy had to be Tanner's. And it was time he had a talk with his son.

The next day Bryce took Tanner out for breakfast. On the way, his father had been quieter than usual, so it was a relief to Diesel when they ordered, and Bryce finally said, "Son, I asked you to breakfast because I have something serious to tell you, and I wanted to do it early, before you have to go to the base and have other things to focus on."

"Are you all right, dad?" Tanner grew serious. "Is it your health?"

"No, no." Bryce waved that away with his hand. "Nothing like that."

Tanner sat back in his chair, relieved. Whatever his dad had to say, everything would be fine.

Nothing to worry about.

If his dad's health was good, everything would be okay. His dad had no idea of the things Diesel had seen and had done under orders. Things a civilian might worry about were easy, compared to those life-or-death situations the SEALs lived in and around. He took a sip of his coffee, ready to listen.

"You've slept with a lot of women, according to your brother, Andy."

"A few." Diesel wondered where this was going. Was his dad going to ask him about sex? Or picking up women?

"Locally, too, I imagine."

"Yes, a few live here." Diesel hoped his dad didn't want to be fixed up with a local woman he knew. He hoped it wasn't that because he might not be okay with that.

Bryce cleared his throat. "Good." He took a swallow of his coffee and then continued, "I was in the park the other day and saw a young woman with a small child who was playing."

Diesel nodded, wishing his dad would get to the point and stop dragging his feet with whatever he had to say. *Out with it, dad* was what he wanted to say, but instead he just nodded, giving his dad the time and respect, he deserved.

"Her little boy is two years old, and he looks and sounds just like you. So much, he could be a clone of you at that age."

"Really?" Diesel frowned and tried to think back two years to remember if he'd been dating anyone local that year.

"Yes. And I want you to take this seriously."

Diesel nodded. He had slept with several local women, but not in that year. They all wanted to chase him into their beds, so they could brag that they'd slept with a SEAL. He'd enjoyed the excess at first, but hook-ups had gotten old quick. He'd stopped dating the locals because they wanted too much permanency and he never stayed around for long.

If he could just meet the perfect woman like that one he'd met at the costume party that time.

Her, he wouldn't have minded seeing more often. Once was not enough.

He sat, thinking. "That year I shipped out November first, and before that, I was dating Kira off and on. But she doesn't have any kids. And she doesn't want them."

"Did you go out with anyone else local that year? Even for one night?"

"No, I didn't..." His voice trailed away as his thoughts began to churn. "Though there was a Halloween party. And a beautiful girl who wouldn't give me her phone number. But that was just one brief evening event."

"So, you didn't sleep with her?"

"We, uh, got together dad. So, technically, yes."

"Then technically, I would say this Pippa is the same girl, and her little boy is your son and my grandson."

Diesel shook his head. "That's crazy."

"No. It's not. And you need to talk to this girl Pippa and meet the boy."

Their food came, and Diesel was suddenly starving. "Let's shelve this for now and dig in," he said. He didn't want the topic to ruin his meal. He'd deal with this later. He needed to eat, and then get back to the base and work.

∼

F ull of boundless energy and the smile and face of a Gerber baby, Pippa often looked at little Bryce, lifted him into the air, and looking into his eyes said, "You're a handsome boy, just like your daddy."

If only she knew who and where his daddy was. He was missing out on seeing this beautiful child grow up. This child, who was now her whole world.

There were only so many SEALs in the world. She just didn't know how to find hers, or if he'd even want to be found.

What if he she found him, and he didn't want anything to do with Bryce? That would break her heart.

S tan Nitty was finally out of prison.

He collected his personal belongings and walked out a free man, after serving half his sentence. He'd been on good behavior and convinced them he had changed and felt remorse for what he'd done. Privately he felt otherwise.

That guy had deserved what he'd gotten and then some. But that was in the past now. Time to move on.

Now, he was out, and things were going to change. He would find Joyce. It was time he got his wife back. He'd been inside the joint a long time without a woman, and he wanted to sink into her softness again and take what was his. Wherever she was, he would find her.

Traveling to the cache he'd hidden in the woods; he was pleased to find his weapons and ammo were still there. He collected them and then set off to the town where Joyce had last been seen. It was time to track down his woman.

4

The search only took Stan a week. Joyce hadn't been very careful, even though she'd changed her name.

Pippa. What a ridiculous name. Her parents were crazy to saddle their daughter with a middle name like Pippalousa. What the hell kind of name was that? Joyce Nitty was her proper name and it was time she took her proper name back.

His former cellmate knew a guy who could find anyone. Everyone left an electronic trail of some kind. It had taken the guy just two days to find Joyce, now calling herself Pippa. She lived in Virginia and was working at a grocery store there.

Maybe his wife thought he couldn't find her after he was sent to prison. Or maybe she thought he'd give up. But he would never give up on taking back what was his.

Now that he'd found her, he couldn't believe his eyes. She had fuller curves than she'd had before. Bigger breasts which was good. But she was there in the park with a toddler around two years of age. And that little boy had just called her mama.

A little boy with dark curly hair and brown eyes. The

boy that looked nothing like him. And anyone who could count would know that the child couldn't possibly be his.

So, the bitch had spread her legs for another man. And now, she had a baby. A boy. She'd let some other man fuck her, and then had a son that should've been his.

How dare she.

He'd picked her out especially to be his. She'd been young and beautiful and untouched. A virgin. She should've been popping out sons every couple of years to carry on the Nitty name. Little Stan juniors he could teach to hunt and fish. Now, she'd tainted herself.

He was so angry he couldn't see straight. When he got his hands on her, he'd make her pay. Before, he would've tried to woo her. He'd daydreamed of that and of keeping her naked in bed to please him. But all that was over now.

She wanted to behave like a slut, so now she'd be treated like one. And she'd just given him the best way possible to control her. Because he knew his wife remembered the feel of the back of his hand.

And she loved children.

She'll do anything to make sure nothing happens to that little boy.

Pippa pushed Bryce on the baby swings and laughed as he kicked his legs out and squealed. He loved going as high as she was willing to push him, and she had the feeling he would have taken off and flown if he could have.

Like his daddy. Probably.

It wasn't the first time she'd had that thought. She guessed that he took after his daddy in much more than looks.

If only she knew more about his daddy. In particular where he was and what he would think about having a son.

She dared not hope to run into him in this town full of SEALs and she'd given up praying for that. It felt like no one was listening. Or if listening, not inclined to answer her prayer with the answer she desired.

Sometimes she wasn't sure what she desired. She only wanted him found if it would be good for their son. If not, then she'd rather he be kept away.

Maybe this was for the best after all.

She and Bryce were both happy. In fact, Bryce was one of the happiest toddlers she'd ever seen. He never threw a tantrum or cried or reached for things he couldn't have.

Pippa tried to do the same.

She would not cry one more tear into her pillow over her situation. She'd been blessed with a healthy son who she loved with all her heart.

That would have to be enough.

S tan watched Joyce for two weeks to find her patterns, so he'd know the best place to make a grab and go.

He'd lined the van to soundproof it and darkened the windows. He'd bought toys and had a special juice he'd mixed himself, for the kid. All kids liked juice, and this one, mixed with that cherry children's cough syrup, would make the kid sleep. He didn't want to have to listen to or deal with the kid.

Surprised to see her leaving work early today, he chose to follow her.

She'd changed the pattern. But that could be good if no one was expecting her so early.

He parked down the street and watched her go into her

apartment, and then watched the sitter come out, get in her car, and drive away.

The timing was right. He felt it in every cell of his body as he moved the van to the graveled area behind the apartment building and parked. Exiting, he made his way to her door.

Didn't take much to break in, as flimsy as the locks were and no deadbolt on.

For someone who'd run away to Virginia and changed her name to hide, she wasn't very safety-conscious in her own apartment.

He moved into the apartment, quiet and slow, listening.

She was in her bedroom, humming a song for the kid, who was singing nonsense words to her tune.

Had it been his kid, he would've told her to cut that shit out. Boys didn't need to learn that stuff. He'd raise his boys the way his daddy had raised him, so they'd grow up tough and hard and not be mama's boys.

He had a feeling this kid was going to be a screamer. Kids screaming in restaurants and out in public drove him nuts. No way was he going to listen to that in the van.

He stepped into the room and moved quietly behind her.

She was putting the squirming kid into pajamas while the kid clearly didn't want to be still that long. She was too busy and focused on her kid to notice Stan.

Then he was right behind her.

His hands were on her, one over her mouth and the other around her neck.

He knew how to make her pass out, and once out, she'd be like a ragdoll, easy to tie and carry. Within minutes, he had her trussed up and slung over his shoulder.

The boy started crying and reaching up for his mama.

Stan ignored him.

All kids cried, and the neighbors would've heard it before.

In the living room, he laid her down on the couch, and then went back for the boy.

The boy was still crying out for his mama, tears running and a bubble forming under his nose.

Snotty nosed kid.

Stan pulled the water bottle out of his pocket and opened it; ready to pour the juice into one of those kiddie sippy cups he'd seen on the table by the bed. Taking the lid off, he saw it was empty. He poured in the juice.

The kid had quieted, watching him. He then toddled over and reached for the cup.

"Juice," he said.

So, the kid could talk some.

"Yeah. Juice." He handed the kid the cup.

The boy started to take a drink. Then he remembered his mother. "Mama," he said, and he toddled into the other room to look for her. "Mama."

Stan followed the kid into the living room carrying the cup. "Mama is sleeping. Taking a nap." He held out the cup. "Here's your juice."

The boy took the cup, and then carrying it, went over to his mother and laid his head down on her arm, still holding the cup, which now tipped, leaking juice out on the floor.

"Mamma, night, night," he said, his head still next to his mama as he patted her with his other hand.

"She's tired," Stan said. "Drink your juice."

The boy picked his head up, looked at Stan for a minute, and then took another drink.

How long was it going to take the kid to drink that juice? Too long already.

His patience was already shot.

Damn kid.

If he didn't need the kid to control his wife, he'd have taken care of the kid right now. One way or another. But for now, he was stuck with him.

"Drink your juice all gone and you can have a cookie," he said. He did have a cookie in his jacket pocket, but the kid would be asleep before he got a chance to eat it.

~

Pippa didn't hear him until his hands were on her mouth and her neck, cutting off her air and making everything go black. The last thing she remembered was her son's face, looking up at her as her ex-husband's voice said in her ear, "I've waited years for you. But you couldn't wait on your husband. I'm back, and the waiting is over."

Then she went out like a light.

She woke, looking for her son and not seeing anything but the darkness in the van.

Stan was driving.

Is he drunk? He used to drink and drive.

If Bryce was in the van, she hoped Stan wasn't drunk.

Where's Bryce?

She hoped he hadn't hurt her baby boy.

"You're awake and probably wondering where that little boy is right now," Stan said. "I'm taking good care of him. And I'll continue to take good care of him — if you don't give me any trouble."

He'd gagged her, and she couldn't speak, so she had no way to answer him.

Turning up the radio, he started singing to "Patience" by Guns N' Roses. She didn't know if that was supposed to be for her benefit or his.

She glared at him because she couldn't speak and thought, *Let the mind games begin. Only this time you won't win because I'm stronger than I used to be. And now I have a son to be strong for.*

She tried to focus on where he might be taking them. Tried to listen for sounds. To feel the direction of the vehicle. But it was no use. And she'd been knocked out for she didn't know how long.

What if no one knows we are gone? What if they don't even know to look for us?

5

Diesel and his father were able to track down the mystery woman by using her license plate number, which his father had written down after she'd driven away from the park with her son.

Possibly his son.

Unsure of how to approach her, he'd decided on the direct approach. Too much time had passed since they'd met—if this was truly the mystery woman he'd dreamed about so many nights away in other countries, doing his job. If she was his fairy princess and her son was his baby, dancing around it would just waste more time.

If the boy was his son, he didn't want to waste another minute.

Now he stood outside Pippa's apartment, ringing the bell, but no one answered the door.

Then he loudly knocked three times.

She wasn't home.

He'd have to adapt and adjust his plan. He went back down the stairs, got in his truck, and headed for the grocery where she worked.

Intel he and his father had gathered said she worked six

days a week at the grocery store checking groceries, and then took a night class from seven to eight-thirty on Monday, Wednesday, and Friday nights. It being Wednesday, and nearly seven, she should've been home from the grocery by now to leave her son with the sitter.

Her pattern was broken.

Diesel scowled at the clock and wondered what had caused her to change her pattern.

Starting the truck, he backed out of the parking lot and headed for the grocery. He'd have to see if she was still at work, and if she wasn't, he'd ask if she'd been at work today and when she'd left.

She wouldn't have gone to class with her son. The course she was taking was court transcription, and there'd be no way she could do that with a child in her arms.

Maybe the boy was sick, and she'd taken him to urgent care.

He hoped nothing bad had happened to either of them. But he was getting that feeling in the pit of his stomach when something went wrong. And that feeling, which was battle-tested, had never been wrong. Not even once. He'd learned long ago to trust his gut. The more the minutes ticked on, the more his gut was sending out those warning signals.

Driving to the grocery store, the feelings only increased.

He parked, walked inside, and looked for the manager.

The man was in his office on the phone.

Diesel waited for him to hang up. When he did, Diesel said, "I'm concerned about my friend, Pippa. She works here as a checker."

The manager frowned and said, "Concerned? Why?"

"She didn't arrive home tonight."

"Who are you?"

"A friend of Pippa's. She usually comes home, and then

goes to that class she's taking after the sitter arrives, but she never came home tonight."

Concern for Pippa changed the manager's facial expression and body language. It also redirected his attention to finding her. "Did you try her cellphone?" He had his phone in his hand and started to dial. "I sent her home an hour early because we were slow, and I had too many checkers standing around. She should've been home a long time ago."

The phone went immediately to voice mail, and the man's frown deepened. "She's not answering. She must not have her phone turned on." He shook his head. "That's not something she does because of Bryce; in case the sitter has to call her. She never turns off her phone."

Diesel froze.

Bryce? That was his father's name. *When were you going to give me that bit of Intel, dad?*

The manager was looking at him strangely. "Who did you say you were again?" he asked.

"I didn't." He pulled out his I.D. showing his name and his military credentials, what he was able to divulge about himself.

"And you know Pippa how?"

"I believe I may be the boy's father, and I believe something has happened to Pippa."

The manager started dialing the phone again. "I'm calling the police."

"Good. You do that." Diesel then went silent. He'd be gone before they ever got there. Disappearing was something he excelled at. Infiltration was a specialty of his. But searching for, hunting for anyone or anything, for that he'd call on his SEAL brother, Osprey, who was the best hunter he knew.

He was out the door and on his phone to Osprey before

the manager even finished the call to the police. And within just a couple minutes, he was gone, as if he'd never been there.

Retracing her probable and usual route from her work to home, he talked to Osprey, explaining the situation.

"Give me every bit of info you have, down to the smallest detail, even if it appears unimportant," Osprey said. "You going to her apartment to search?"

"Headed there now." If there was anything in her apartment that could clue them in on where she might've gone, he would find it.

At her apartment again, he ran up the apartment steps all the way to the top floor without being out of breath and stopped at her door. He tried the door, believing it would be locked, thinking he might have to break it down to get in, but it swung open with an easy push.

Damn. If he'd done that when he was here before, he wouldn't have wasted time at the grocery store.

The door squeaked, and he scanned the first room and then stepped inside.

There'd been a struggle.

A table lamp lay broken on the floor, a bowl of cereal O's had spilled and scattered all over the floor. A child's juice cup, which must've been Cranapple, or berry had spilled onto the beige carpet, leaving a stain which reminded him too much of fresh blood.

Though it wasn't blood. He'd seen plenty of spilled blood and knew exactly what the color of blood looked like, and whether it was freshly spilled or blood that had been there a while. He bent down.

This spill was recent enough to have been early evening.

She'd come home and shortly afterward; someone had taken them both.

He moved to the kitchen just off the first room. Clean,

nothing spilled or broken there. Remarkably clean for having a baby in the house.

Her purse sat on a kitchen chair. He went over to it and looked inside. If her cell phone was inside and turned off, he'd have his answer to why a call wouldn't go through.

No cellphone.

He moved into the bedroom, and then the bathroom. Nothing looked out of place in either.

In her bedroom, a crib was set up in the corner, and her bed took up the middle of the room. A changing table stood next to the crib. No longer in use, she now used it as storage, and piles of neatly folded baby clothes sat on top of it.

Back in the front room again, he noted there was no television, no radio, just books and a basket with yarn and crochet hooks, and toys for toddlers.

Her life centered around her child. Everything about the place said a mother and her baby lived here.

He felt very much out of place here. Like an intruder. Which he was.

He'd entered many homes before, some with women and children. But he'd never felt so much like an intruder until now. This woman was trying to create a good home for her son.

His son if he was to believe his father.

Before his dad had flown back home, he'd suddenly turned detective and decided to find out about the woman and the baby.

According to the friend Pippa worked with, Pippa didn't know who the father was.

If Pippa was the woman he thought she was, then there was a very good reason she might say she didn't know who the father was. She didn't know his name. And he hadn't known hers.

Until recently.

He could've been angry with her about having the baby and not telling him, except for those facts.

But if she was hiding because she didn't want to tell him, that was something else. And if that were the reason, then he'd have more than a few words to say to her about that.

Fathers had rights, too, and his son was not going to grow up without his father in his life. No way in hell.

Between his connections and his SEAL training she hadn't stood much chance of hiding from him, if hiding was what she was trying to do. Even though, technically speaking, SEALs weren't supposed to be digging around on their own time and using government resources and manpower to achieve their own goals.

Pippa's friend Cheryl had told his dad that Pippa had been trying to hide from an ex who might hurt her if he found her. An ex who was not only an ex-husband but was an inmate in prison.

Matt, who was a computer genius and had an uncanny ability of being able to find almost anyone, had turned up the fact that Stan Nitty had just been released from prison a few weeks ago.

Even if Pippa wasn't the woman his dad now insisted she was, and the boy wasn't his son, she still needed to know her ex was free again, so she'd be aware. For her own safety and precautions.

No court-ordered document would protect her if a violent man like her ex came after her.

Diesel had seen the pictures of Pippa, which were part of the divorce proceedings. The marks upon Pippa's neck made him want to do bad things to Stan Nitty.

No man should ever beat or injure his wife. That kind of thing made Diesel's blood boil.

Nitty was a dangerous man and if he decided to come after Pippa, she'd be in danger.

Diesel wasn't about to let anything happen to Pippa, whether the boy was his or not. It would give him immense pleasure to wipe scum like her ex off the face of the earth.

No woman deserved to be treated they way Pippa had been.

Court documents had been easy to find and read. It was all there. The pictures of her neck where the man had squeezed showed bruises shaped like finger marks.

He couldn't keep those images out of his head.

Diesel would take pleasure in breaking every one of the man's fingers and showing him just what that squeezing would've felt like to his wife. And Diesel knew how to exact pain without killing. Though he was a trained killer, courtesy of the United States government, killing would be too fast for scum like Pippa's ex. The man had served time for felonious assault and was now out of prison.

No one seemed to know where he currently was, but he'd been sighted outside of Ohio, so he wasn't staying put and checking in with his probation office.

The man was on the move.

And Pippa and her son were missing.

Had her ex tried to contact Pippa? Had he found her?

If the scumbag had found her, he'd find the boy, too. Which meant the boy might be in danger.

Diesel needed to find Pippa, and *now*.

6

After driving the route, Pippa would have taken, more than once, and going over her apartment, Diesel was at a dead end. He drove onto the base, and ran over everything again in his head.

It was time to call Rich, and to see if any of his brothers were free to help him find the mysterious woman of his dreams, who seemed to keep slipping through his fingers.

He made the call, and the answer didn't surprise him.

SEALs were brothers and looked after their own. And that included their family members.

Rich was the first to step up, before Diesel even had to ask. "Hell, yeah, we're with you on this. And we'll find her, brother. You know as a team we're unbeatable." Rich added, "Come over to Chicks. Many of us are already here."

Turning around, Diesel drove off the base again, and headed to Chick's Bar. He made record time and managed to avoid a traffic ticket.

Inside, several of the men were seated at the table. Rich, Osprey, and Kik sat, having a beer.

"We have a potential team of six," Rich said. He gestured to the men. "You have us. R.T. and Cutter want in, but we don't really need six. Three is enough. So Matt is going to stay on base, but stay in contact. Cutter will jump in, and do perimeter patrol, if needed. We three are the extraction team."

"Four," Diesel said crossing his arms.

The men noted his body language, and knew not to argue with him. This was likely his son they were rescuing, along with the boy's mother. Of course, Diesel would insist on being in.

Matt, R.T. and Cutter joined them at the bar.

"We'll find her quicker than anyone else could," Rich said.

Matt nodded in agreement. An expert in computer skills, Matt could hack into any computer, and find out anything.

And Osprey? He lived for the hunt. Game, people, anything he set his sights on as his intended target, he found, took down, and he delivered what he targeted. "We'll find them."

Diesel didn't know of any other men more qualified to help him right now, than these six SEAL brothers. He couldn't have done better if he'd picked them himself.

Popping another antacid, he went quiet. He grabbed another, eating them like candy.

"You all right, brother?" R.T. clapped a hand on his shoulder. "Never seen you need those before." He gave a friendly squeeze saying, "You know you could sit this one out, and let us handle it. You're too close to it."

Diesel shook his head. "No way."

"All right, then. Let's go for a thirty-minute run. You've got to do something, while you wait. Matt will let us know, as soon as he has something," R.T. said.

"You know it," Matt said, picking up his to go order. "I'm heading back to the base now, and will be on my computer shortly."

If there was a way to track someone online, Matt had the skills to do it. Matt had tracked down Pippa's ex using his well-honed computer skills, and now he'd narrowed her possible location down to a house on the outskirts of town, which appeared, at first, to be abandoned.

Stan Nitty had saved whatever money he'd gotten from the sale of the house he'd shared with Pippa, and had taken a portion of it to buy a run-down house on the edge of Virginia.

～

Diesel and the team surrounded the house, and watched for less than an hour, though it seemed much longer to him.

Minutes had never crawled so slow in his life.

They waited for the sun to go down, so they could use their night vision goggles to see who might be inside and where.

At first glance, the house appeared abandoned. But SEALs knew appearances could be deceiving.

At last, the sun went down, and they donned their night vision to do a visual search, from a distance that wouldn't give away their positions.

No lights shined in the windows, and no sounds could be heard.

Until the child started crying.

Diesel froze.

The sound tore at his heart in a way nothing ever had before.

That was his son. Dammit, he just knew it.

The first sound he'd ever heard from his son, and it was a sound of distress.

It almost made him frantic. He had to reach the boy. To

59

save him from whatever was happening to him right now, or what might happen to him.

But he also had to stay calm, focused, stay on the goal, and the mission. Keep his head clear from emotion to do his job. This might be the hardest mission he'd ever been on.

Most of the time SEALs lived for the next mission, but this was one mission he wished had never happened.

His little boy should've been safe at home, playing with his toys, being doted on by his loving family. Not trapped in a damn shack by some lunatic who wouldn't let his ex-wife go.

His child, who he'd never once held in his arms, needed him.

The urge to charge in immediately, to destroy the man who'd abducted the child, and the child's mother, was so strong it made him want to do *something*.

He tamped that down, controlled it. Forced it to bend to his will. He had to do what was best for the boy, for the safety of the boy, for the complete success of this mission.

There could be no mistakes. Failure was unacceptable.

"You're too close to this," Rich said softly.

"Don't even think of telling me to sit this one out," Diesel said. "That's not an option."

"We won't fail," Rich said. "He's one man against six SEALs."

Lights in the house turned on, in the kitchen, now that it was dark. Up to this point the woman and child were in the kitchen, and the man had been moving in and out of it.

After the boy started crying, the lights in the kitchen were turned on.

Patiently the team waited for Nitty to move away from the woman, and child, into another room. They wouldn't chance the boy, or the woman, getting hurt but would wait for the right moment.

Trained SEALs were used to waiting and spent far more time waiting during an op than most people would have guessed.

Real life opps were not like Hollywood movies.

Finally Nitty moved down the hall, into a back bedroom, and Rich signaled to the team to move closer to the house.

Diesel and his team moved closer, watching as they moved.

Cutter would stay outside, on perimeter watch, and would communicate any movements, as he didn't have to remove his night vision goggles.

Nitty was in one of the bedrooms cleaning his gun.

Pippa was in the kitchen, seated on a chair, and tied to it.

Little Bryce was playing with a toy car, rolling it back and forth, along the floor.

Diesel took all this in.

God, he could kill for what was happening to Pippa.

What I wouldn't give to be sitting on a kitchen floor playing cars and trucks with my son.

He took a breath and gritted his teeth.

Focus. On. The. Mission.

Then it was on.

The team moved without speaking, using hand signals. One, then two, then three, and then they were go - into the house, and moving to reach the one man they wanted to take out.

Rich moved in through the front door, gun ready.

The first room was dark and empty. He removed his night vision, and pulled a black ski mask over his face, so no one would recognize him.

Kik followed him and repeated his movements.

Diesel was third, and seeing everything through his night vision as they all were, until they pulled the goggles up, and the ski masks down, the only sound in their earpieces was their breathing.

Without their night vision, they'd have to rely on Cutter and Osprey's eyes, as they patrolled outside the house.

"Nitty, back bedroom. Just laid his gun down reaching for something on closet self. Go, go, go!

Nitty reached for a box on the closet shelf. He'd laid his gun on the bed.

R.T. brought up the rear, and Diesel could hear him breathing heavier than usual. He'd mentioned allergies earlier, and said he needed to take his meds when they were in route.

It sounded much too loud to Diesel, but then his nerves were on edge, worried about his son. Staying cool was taking lots more effort than any op had ever required.

Rich moved silent and quick, toward the back bedroom Stan Nitty was in.

The man had put down his gun to reach for a box, so his hands were up.

There was no better moment to go. This should be a quick in, and out, as the man had no idea they were there.

Then R.T. sneezed.

Nitty turned toward the door, dropping the box, and grabbed for his rifle.

He fired and one shot hit the door trim, beside Kik's head, splintering the wood.

Rich, calm and cool, shot Nitty in the shoulder of his shooting arm, knocking him backward against the closet door.

Nitty looked down, shock flooding his face, on seeing that he'd been shot, and blood was now staining his shirt. "Who the hell are you?" he asked.

Not one of them answered. He'd get no Intel from them.

Nitty had a stockpile of weapons and ammunition, but

he was just one man, and one man with a loaded gun, or even with multiple guns was no match for a team of trained SEAL's.

The entire operation was over in less than ten minutes.

Kik wrapped an arm around Nitty's neck, and then applied pressure, and Nitty soon slumped.

Stan Nitty now lay on the ground, passed out.

Diesel hurried into the kitchen, took one look at Pippa, and said, "Are you hurt?"

Then he bent down on one knee, to untie Pippa from the chair she was tied to.

Pippa heard the voice behind her, and chills ran down her back. She knew that voice, behind her ear.

I know that voice. From one night. One wonderful night I could never forget.

The man dressed all in black military clothing and gear, like a commando out of some movie, knelt in front of her, and started untying her hands.

A long white scar peaked out from his right sleeve. She'd seen that scar before.

Could it really be him? She knew that scar.

He was working the knots loose, with quick and sure hands, and a calm, strong presence.

She knew that voice.

My gladiator. He's here. Am I dreaming?

She realized she hadn't answered him yet.

"No," she said in a soft whisper. "He hasn't hurt us yet. But he was going to."

"No," he said. "He wouldn't. I wouldn't have let him."

She drew a shuddering breath. "How did you find me?"

It all seemed like something out of a fairy tale, the way he'd suddenly appeared. The hero of her dreams was flesh and blood, and right in front of her.

She couldn't help staring.

He'd untied her, and now he pulled his goggles up, so as not to scare the boy, as he moved around in front of the chair where the boy played. Then he bent down on one knee again, and looked at the boy.

Bryce looked up at him, smiled the sweet smile only a two-year-old can give, and then said, "Play trucks."

It was a command. Not so unlike his father's.

Tears filled Pippa's eyes. "I have something to tell you."

Diesel turned his brown eyes to took into hers, and her son turned to watch her, too. He knew what she was going to say, but he needed her to say it.

He needed her to tell him what she should have told him a long time ago.

"We made a beautiful boy one night. I'm glad you'll be able to meet him now. I'm glad you found us. Thank you for saving our lives." Tears started rolling down her cheeks, and that was all she could get out.

Diesel had tears in his eyes now, too.

How could he be angry with her, when he'd looked into her eyes, and seen the feelings and emotions there? The way she loved and cared for their son?

Our son.

It really was true. Not some fairytale, or imagined thing from his father.

The old man knew. From the moment he saw little Bryce, he knew.

A little hand patted Diesel's rock-hard thigh, and he turned his head to look at his son again.

"Play trucks now," he demanded.

He and Pippa both laughed, as they looked at their son.

"How about we go home, and play trucks there," Diesel said.

But Bryce was already playing trucks by driving the truck up Diesels black boot.

Diesel had a grin from ear to ear, so big that his face was hurting. He looked at the other team members, who'd gathered in the room.

"I have a son," he said.

"Looks just like you," Kik said.

"Stubborn like you, too," Rich said.

"Bring that boy on out here, where I can see him," Cutter said. He was outside, guarding their prisoner, Stan.

"Let's go meet Cutter," Diesel said.

He held out a hand to help Pippa up, and she stood, moving her arms and legs, getting the circulation moving again.

She went to pick up Bryce, but Diesel said, "Let me."

He reached his arms toward the boy, waiting to see if Bryce would come to him, and grinned even wider when he did. Lifting him up, into his arms, he held him, and blinked a few times to clear the sudden moisture which affected his vision.

They walked out of the house into the yard where Cutter was watching Stan.

Still out, he looked less dangerous to Pippa, especially with SEALs on her side, and in control.

Stan couldn't hurt her now.

"We've talked about the way this needs to go down from here," Rich said. "Since this was an unauthorized op. We're going to fade into the background. What we need for you to do, is call the police from here, using this phone."

He handed her Stan's cellphone. "Tell them he abducted you, tell them exactly what happened, up until we arrived. Leave out the part where he had you tied up. We can't be here when they arrive, and you can't mention us. It's got to be as if we were never here."

"Okay." She nodded. "I can do that."

"When you call the police, tell them he's been shot, and

may need an ambulance. You didn't stay, because you were in fear of your life, if he came to again."

"Now, here's the story you need to tell. He had you in this house, and was threatening to kill you. You saw a chance to take his gun, and shoot him, and you took it. Then you grabbed your baby, and ran like hell. Used his van to drive yourself away from him, and back home."

"But I don't know how to shoot a gun, especially one of those big things."

"Give her a quick lesson, Diesel." Kik said. "Just enough that she'd know how to pick it up, and pull the trigger."

He held out the gun used to shoot Nitty toward Pippa. "The gun is clean and empty at the moment, so it's safe, but now we want your prints on it, so go ahead and take it."

"Hold it like this," Diesel showed her, using his own gun. "When you shoot, you'd pull this trigger."

When she hesitated, he said, "It's not going to hurt you. We're having you dry fire first, that means no ammo. It's just to get your prints on it."

She copied everything he did.

Then he loaded it, and had her place the gun against her shoulder, and fire into the woods.

The recoil hurt her shoulder, and she was sure she'd bruise.

This was the first time she'd ever shot a gun.

Being married to Stan had made her nervous around guns, and she'd never wanted to learn.

He'd been happy to keep her ignorant of her own self-defense, and dependent upon him. In fact, he encouraged her fear of guns.

It was just one more way to control her.

Done with the quick shooting lesson, she handed the gun back to Kik, who still had his gloves on.

Kik took the gun, and went to prepare the scene.

"I'm scared," she said. "What do I tell the police again? Won't they arrest me, and take the baby?"

"That's not going to happen. When you call in, tell them you want to charge him with kidnapping you and your son, and that you were terrified for your life. He tried to choke you to death once. And that's on record. This time you shot in self-defense, and got away. With his record, they'll send him back to prison, and he won't get to you again."

"But what if he gets out again?"

"I'll be there," Diesel said. "He's not ever going to get to you, or Bryce again, but even if on some wild chance he does, I'll be there."

He'd be there? What exactly did he mean?

Her heart thumped hard inside her chest.

"Thank you," she said. "Thank you, all of you. I don't know what I'd have done if he'd hurt Bryce."

"It's over now," Diesel said.

"Time to go." Rich tapped his watch.

R.T. carried Stan's limp body inside, to arrange it, and came back out carrying the ropes used to tie Pippa to the chair.

"Why aren't you leaving them?" Pippa asked.

"Doesn't fit the story," R.T. said, and then winked. He tossed the ropes into an SUV, and climbed in.

"Make that call," Rich said.

She took the phone, and called the police, following their instructions.

"Here are the van keys," Cutter said, tossing them to her.

"I've got Bryce," Diesel said. "There's no car seats, so I'll buckle him into the passenger seat."

Pippa wished there was a back seat, but Stan had stripped it out, so he could toss them into the back of the van, close to the driver's seat where he could watch them.

She watched Diesel strapping their son in, as careful as any other dad.

This all still seemed unreal, like a dream she hadn't woke up from yet.

"R.T. and I are going to tail you back to your apartment, and wait out of sight, until the police leave. Then we'll go get my truck, and talk."

She nodded, her gaze clinging to his face.

Lord, he was more handsome than she'd known.

"I guess we have a lot to talk about."

"We do. For now, let's stay on track here. You get this van to the apartment, with all the evidence inside, and they'll come here, and go over this place with a fine-tooth comb. All you'll have to do is sit tight at home, and take care of Bryce."

"Sounds good."

Going around to the driver's side, she climbed in. When she started the van and pulled out, a dark SUV slowly pulled out behind her.

R.T. and Diesel would be behind her, though soon they were out of sight. Still, she felt safer knowing they were there.

7

———

The police had come and gone for two days, taking statements, and collecting evidence. Pippa had to tell her story repeatedly and wished that it would all be over soon.

Everyone agreed it was likely Stan would be sent back to prison with a much longer sentence this time.

Her boss had given her time off, and she'd also taken a week off from her classes. Since she hadn't missed any days, losing one week wouldn't be enough to affect her grades.

Everyone was being nice to her and to Bryce, showing their concern, but she was tired of going over the story again, and again. She just wanted it to be over.

It had been over a week now, and though they knew the police would still be keeping an eye on the case, and any odd behavior she might do; it was finally okay for Diesel to start coming around.

He'd begun by showing up, when there were witnesses, introducing himself to her, as if they hadn't just met at the crime scene where he and the other SEALs had saved her life. He hadn't told her he was coming, so her surprise was more genuine.

Everyone seemed to take it as believable, that seeing

them on the news had made him realize the boy might be his.

Even a few of the police officers were encouraging the romance.

A winsome two-year-old, a woman who needed rescuing, and a military hero, well that kind of love story, who could argue against that.

At last, Diesel and Pippa were alone. Or as alone as a single mother with a two-year-old could be. Bryce was napping, and they had a chance to really talk now.

They'd been talking for the better part of an hour.

"Are you sure you want to be a part of our lives? I mean, you hardly know us," her voice was serious, but uncertain.

"I know I dreamed about you, many nights, when I was deployed over the last two years." He reached out a hand for hers, grasped it, and pulled her nearer.

"I dreamed of you too," she smiled. "My gladiator."

He smiled, and continued. "I dreamed of you, and of finding you. Dreamed of making love to you, again. Of touching your skin, kissing your lips. Of sliding my arms around your waist, just like this." His arms slid around her waist.

"Of tasting you again, and again." He kissed her lips softly, and then released her, to finish what he'd waited so long to say. "Of making love to you, all night, and waking up with you still in my bed, in my arms. For two years, I've thought of finding you. Now, you're here."

His arms pulled her closer, until their hips met, and he felt the softness of her fuller, more rounded belly since having the baby, as he looked down into her eyes. "And I don't want to let you go."

Her gaze searched his, looking for what lay deep within, below the surfaces. "Is it only sex?" she asked, "I desire you, I dream of you too, but is it only sex?"

"If it were, any woman would do. No, it isn't only sex. I want you." His eyes searched hers now, seeking his answers. "And I'm hoping you want me, too."

"I do," she breathed the words out. "I want to know you. More and more, to know you. But I'm afraid."

"What are you afraid of?"

Her lips trembled. "That you'll change. And then, you'll hurt me."

"Because of him," he said softly.

"Yes."

He sighed. "Do you know how to conquer a fear?"

She shook her head, unable to speak. Her wide green eyes watched him.

"You conquer a fear by working through it. By facing the fear, and then moving through it. The way out of fear is *through*. It's how you get to the other side."

She nodded, listening.

"We can take this slow. We *should* take this slow. It would be best for you, and for Bryce, too," Diesel said.

"Yes," she said quickly.

Relief showed on her face.

"I'm not going to push you to chose me. I want you to choose me for me, and I want to choose you for you, neither of us owning the other. Bryce has been fatherless for two years already, and I'll be in his life now, no matter what you decide, but neither of you know me that well, not yet. This will take time."

She gave him a little smile. "Bryce is the easy one, I think. Children just love right away, like puppies. It's so innocent and pure. First loves are like that, too. We go into them wide-eyed and thinking no one will hurt us, no one will leave us. And then, they do." Pippa stared off, away from him.

"Pippa," he said softly. "I would injure *myself* before I

would ever hurt you or Bryce. I'm not the kind of man who hurts women, or children. I'm a protecting kind of man, the kind who saves them."

"Yes, you are," she smiled a soft smile. "You certainly saved me. And Bryce, too."

"How about we start with this? I want to protect you and Bryce, for the rest of my life. To make sure no harm comes to you. But I want more."

"More?" she whispered the word.

"Yes. More. I want to be the protector of your heart."

She breathed in sharply, and held her breath.

"Will you allow me to do that for you? To guard and protect your heart?"

This was beyond anything she'd ever dreamed of. It hardly seemed real.

She placed her hand on his warm, strong forearm. Feeling his strength in body, and the strength of his love, and this gift he was giving her now.

"Yes," she breathed out. "Yes."

Though they would marry nine months later, with a daughter on the way, both considered the day of that first vow to be their first wedding day, when Diesel became her protector, and the guardian and keeper of her heart.

THE END

SAMPLE CHAPTER: REAL MOVIE HERO, CHAPTER ONE, LITTLE CREEK, VIRGINIA

Reed "Railroad" Tindal aka "R.T." sat outside, on the deck of Chicks bar at the marina, enjoying his beer, as he and two of his SEAL brothers watched a boat pulling into one of the slips.

It was a perfect evening for sailing. Just enough of a breeze and the sun starting to set.

"That's the life," "Cutter" Antonious (Tony) said. "What I'm going to do, after I retire. Nothing but sails, suds, and sweethearts."

"A girl for you in every port," Tanner "Diesel" Taylor said. "Not much different from what you have now."

Diesel liked to have a beer in every port, but Cutter, he was all about the women.

Around SEALs there were always women. Drawn to them like moths to flames.

A seagull landed on one of the posts nearby and looked at them for food.

Sheri, the cheerful, dimpled waitress showed up again, to see if they wanted another beer.

"Fred has joined your party," she said. "Do you want some pretzels for him? And another beer?"

Reed shook his head. "Sorry, guys, I'd hang for another beer, and to stay and chat," Reed said, "but I'm headed out to see a movie premiere."

"Oh, lucky you," Sheri said.

"Which one?" Diesel asked.

"*Turn and Deliver*, with Cole Kennick," Reed said.

"He's very handsome," Sheri said. "I like his movies."

"There should be plenty of good action scenes in that one," Cutter said. He raised his nearly empty glass. "And I'll take another beer, hun."

She smiled her dimpled grin at him. "You've got it."

"He does a better job keeping it real than most do," Reed said.

"How'd you get passes?" Diesel asked.

"Won them from the radio station," Reed said. "I've got one unclaimed pass. If you'd like to go, Sheri."

"You know I can't," Sheri shook her head. "My boyfriend wouldn't like that."

"It's just a movie," Reed said. "Not a kiss."

She put one hand on her hip. "Now you know that movies lead to kisses, and that is how people get into trouble."

"Are you saying you couldn't keep yourself from kissing me?" Reed teased.

Throwing one hand in the air she said, "Now you know that's not what I meant." Shaking her head, she turned and walked away.

"Well, guys, looks like I have one pass up for grabs, if one of you want it," Reed said.

"Can't tonight," Cutter said. "I'm meeting a chick here."

"That does not surprise me," Reed said.

"Another hot dancer with long legs?" Diesel asked.

Cutter grinned. "You know it."

The man was predictable as hell when it came to women, and he always seemed to be dating a dancer.

Reed turned to Diesel. "You want it?"

"Dad is flying in tonight, and I'm picking him up at the airport," Tanner "Diesel" Taylor said. "So this is my limit tonight, and I've got to go." He drained his first beer, and then pushed his chair back to stand.

Reed stood and said good night to both before heading toward the door.

Too bad the extra ticket would go to waste.

He'd just picked the tickets up from the radio station, before heading to Chicks, so there hadn't been time to ask around. Plus, he hadn't figured on both his brothers being busy tonight.

It was a weeknight, not a Saturday, and generally they all hung out at Chicks enjoying the views and brews. Tonight, it had just been the three of them.

It looked like he was headed to the premiere alone. But that didn't bother him. He would enjoy it either way.

****

"I can't go tonight," Tanya told Christie over the phone, her voice hard to hear, while her dog Brutus whined in the background, and Miss Priss meowed mournfully. "There's no way I'll make the movie premiere. I hate to let you down, but it's crazy here."

"Oh, no," Christie said, her stomach dropping to her toes. "What's going on?"

Tanya is bailing.

Dismayed, Christie glanced at her watch.

We are supposed to meet in front of the theater in twenty minutes.

The movie premiere passes Christie had won last week

from the local radio station were only good for tonight's premiere.

It's too late to call someone else. Christie looked down at her red and white dress which showed off her curves.

And I'm dressed forties style.

The whole idea was, she and Tanya were going to have a "girls' night out" dressed in 1940's attire. First, they'd see the movie, and then they'd go for drinks afterward. Both women enjoyed dressing in vintage fashions, and they'd each bought new dresses.

Tanya interrupted Christie's thoughts. "Cole Kennick has to be the hottest man in Hollywood, and you know how much I wanted to go to the premiere with you. But Miss Priss just yakked all over my bedspread right after I finished cleaning up after Brutus. They're both pretty sick. I'm thinking I might need to call the vet."

"I'm so sorry. Are they going to be all right?" Christie's concern for the animals pushed aside her disappointment at her best friend bailing on her. "Do you want me to come over?"

"No, I can handle this," Tanya said. "You go on to the movie. I don't want to be the reason you miss the premiere."

"What do you think it is?" Christie asked. "Did they both get into something? Maybe eat something bad?"

"They've eaten something I didn't give them, that much I do know," Tanya said. "What it is though, I can't tell."

"Oh my god." Christie didn't say her next thought.

Poison. The nasty neighbor might've poisoned them.

Tanya's neighbor was always complaining about Brutus, and his barking.

Brutus was a German Shepard, and very protective of Tanya. Tanya's crazy neighbor jumped at any excuse to call the police.

On the other hand, Miss Priss was a beautiful white

Persian cat who never bothered anyone, although she did shed white hair everywhere.

"You'd better take a sample of the puke to the vet, in case he needs to test what they got into," Christie said.

"Already thought of that. Go enjoy the movie," Tanya said, her tone reassuring. "Don't worry. I don't want to ruin your fun evening."

"You're not going to ruin my evening," Christie said. "But I will miss you."

"Well, you'd better hurry, or you'll be late," Tanya said. "And I don't think they let you in late to premieres."

Christie sighed. "All right, but I'm calling you just as soon as the movie is over."

"Thanks, Christie. And again, I'm so sorry about this."

"It's okay," Christie said. "You just take care of those sweet fur babies."

"Thanks for understanding," Tanya said.

"Hey, that's what best friends do," Christie said.

"Thanks bestie," Tanya said. "Chat soon. Don't be late!"

"I won't, "Christie said. "Bye."

"Bye."

Worrying about Tanya's fur babies, Christie grabbed the movie passes and hurried out the door to her car.

Fortunately, she made every streetlight by driving two miles under the speed limit, and arrived just in time.

The line inside the Cinema One complex was long and filled the lobby. Christie stood at the end of line waiting.

At least I only need one seat.

Two ticket takers stood at the entrance. A man and a woman. The woman held a basket to collect their cell phones. She was explaining that everyone would get their phones back, when they came out of the movie, and she'd be with the phones at all times. Taking the phones was to prevent anyone from sneaking to take a video of the movie.

The woman reminded everyone that pirating was against federal law.

Christie handed the man her pass, and placed her phone into the basket the woman held. As she moved away, her gaze lingered on her phone reluctantly.

I hope Tanya won't need to reach me soon and that the vet tells Tanya her fur babies will be okay.

She's got to do something about that mean neighbor. That woman has gone too far, if she has poisoned them, and I'll bet she has. Poor Miss Priss and Brutus.

Inside, the theater was semi-dark and nearly full.

Christie stood at the bottom of the theater's stadium seating, letting her eyes adjust to the darkness and looking for one good seat.

Oh, there's one next to that fit, handsome man, with the brown hair, wearing the brown leather jacket.

Her gaze stopped and held, as he captured her attention. His build was solid. Strong. Something about him drew her attention—and then she noticed he was looking right back at her, with his intense hazel eyes. But then, his gaze swept past her, to the other side of the theater, as he sat quietly scanning the room.

Is he waiting for someone? Saving that seat? I hope not. It's a good location, and I'm running out of options.

She headed for the seat, hoping it would be free.

Reaching his isle, she leaned forward, drawing his full attention, and asked, "Is this seat taken?"

"No." He shook his head, his eyes watching her.

She smiled, and the teenager seated on the end of the aisle moved his feet, so she could slip between the rows.

"Excuse me," she said, and began the "theater row shuffle," being careful, as she was wearing her highest heels. The new red ones with the little bows on the front and tall, narrow heels.

She'd had so much fun, planning to glam it up on their girls' night out, and both she and Tanya had pretty dresses any pin-up girl would be proud of.

Now, Tanya wouldn't see her, in her new red and white checkered dress. The cool summer dress making her feel attractive and glamorous in a Marilyn Monroe kind of way.

All dolled up for a night on the town, and no one to spend it with.

There was no one here that she knew, to see the dress and appreciate it, along with the time and effort she'd spent on her blonde hairdo and makeup to complete the look.

Plenty of men had ogled her, since she'd stepped out of her car in the theater parking lot, but that wasn't really the kind of attention she wanted.

Tanya would've appreciated the dress, and the time it took to find the perfect dress, and do her hair and makeup just so.

Still, the entire row of men she passed, and men in the rows behind them, watched her every move.

Stepping daintily to the left of the handsome man in the brown leather jacket, and in front of the empty seat, she turned and sat, while trying to play it cool, like she just needed a seat, and not like she'd hoped to sit with him. Wondering where to put her purse, and keeping in mind how a movie theater floor could be sticky, she bent and placed her new, shiny red purse on top of her feet, balancing it on her toes.

The air-conditioning sent a cool draft across her bare shoulders bringing goose bumps and making her want to shiver. She'd forgotten how cool the air could be in a theater when she'd ordered this dress. Wishing she'd worn a shawl; Christie hoped all the people in the theater would create enough body heat to warm the room up. At least when she leaned back against the seat, the vent blew in front of her, not on her back. Though her neck and collarbone were receiving the draft, chilling her front side.

Now that she was seated, she realized how much taller than her the handsome man was. Sitting next to him made her feel downright delicate. His chest, shoulders, and arms were muscular, and he exuded strength.

Oh my, but he's handsome, and he smells good.

She glanced down at his hand.

No wedding ring. I wonder why he's here without a date, or a friend? Women probably fall all over him. I wonder what his name is.

On her other side, a large man in an orange T- shirt and jeans sat holding a huge tub of popcorn. "Here by yourself?" he asked. "That's terrible."

Taken aback by his sly tone, she leaned away from the nosy man, and closer to the handsome man, aware of him now watching her and the nosy man.

"Why would you ask?" she said, frowning, and then catching herself, as she decided she shouldn't be speaking to this stranger about whether she was out alone. "That's none of your business," she said, feeling herself bristle.

Maybe this seat wasn't such a good one after all.

Though the view of the screen was excellent, and she was near enough to the aisle to get out without having to climb over half a row of people, now she hoped the nosy man wouldn't continue to bother her.

Mr. Nosy leaned forward as if to say something else, and his hand reached toward her, but then he stopped, looking past her to handsome man.

She turned to glance at handsome man, wondering what he'd done to stop Mr. Nosy.

Handsome Man's hair was damp, likely from having taken a recent shower. Hot as it was outside, his hair would've dried otherwise.

She became aware once again of his aftershave, or cologne, a manly enticing scent.

"Most people are here because they received a pass to the premiere," the handsome man said dryly.

Mr. Nosy shut up, and went back to eating his popcorn, taking a huge handful.

Christie exhaled stress she didn't know she'd been holding.

Better Mr. Nosy keeps his attention on his popcorn and not on me.

"Thank you," Christie whispered under her breath, just low enough the handsome man could hear.

"No problem," came his low answer.

He smells good.

And that low voice was doing things to her insides as his scent assaulted her senses on another level. Pheromones flooded her body making her aware of her breath, her heartbeat, the way her palms were starting to warm. The slight flush in her pale cheeks and chest, which always happened, would begin now.

Her pheromones could get her into trouble sometimes, when they kicked in before she figured out if a guy was a good man to be with or not.

As the lights began to dim, she thought, *Good thing we'll be in a dark theater. Handsome Man will never know how I'm reacting to him.*

***

Reed Tindal sat scanning the crowd.

Attentiveness was by now an ingrained habit, though he was casual about it, unless he needed not to be.

A trained SEAL, when he was awake, he was always aware of his surroundings.

The pretty blonde, with the creamy skin and stunning green eyes, had caught his attention before she'd noticed him. Then their gazes had connected, and he'd felt that flicker, the one that always happened when attraction kicked in.

This attraction was strong. Strong enough to take him by surprise, as she usually wouldn't have been his type.

She was wearing a delicate red and white checked dress, with little straps, and high heels. With soft blonde shoulder length curls tied with a red ribbon, smokey eyeliner, and cherry red lipstick, she was girly from her head to her red painted toenails, which peeked out of her shoes.

Those red high heeled shoes with red bows on the front were the kind that always made him wonder how a woman would run, if she had to, without turning an ankle. He hoped this beauty never found out.

She turned heads dressed like that, and some heads were best avoided.

He wondered what her story was, and why she was all dressed up to watch a movie by herself. There was a story there. He couldn't imagine any hotblooded male standing up a woman who looked as good as she did.

Reed was used to dating women who were more practical. Sensible about things like shoes, wore jeans instead of dresses, and carried guns.

There was nowhere on that pretty dress where this woman could carry a gun, or anything else. In fact, he'd bet she didn't even know how to shoot a gun.

She looked like the "take care of me" type, not the "I'll take care of things myself" type.

Everyone was seated.

A man in a black suit stepped onto the stage, and welcomed them to the premiere, then the lights were dimmed, and everyone settled in to watch the show.

The blonde, caught up in the story, would catch her breath, only to release it when Cole escaped the bad guy's malevolence, and avoided getting so much as a mark on him. Her breathy sighs and little gasps caught Reed's attention each time, though he was also focusing on the movie.

He was good at doing two things at once. The movie held her complete attention, and she seemed unaware of anything else, though Reed had noted her initial reaction to him.

Reed could have been caught up in the movie as well, if he'd let himself. Cole was one of the few actors who did their own stunts, and he kept his movies more real than most. Which meant Reed didn't disengage and start critiquing action shots five minutes into the movie.

Had he been at home, he might have been as caught up as the woman was. But out in public, nothing would ever take up his total attention. However, that was not to say he wasn't enjoying the movie. In fact, he was enjoying the movie, as well as her reactions to it.

Total opposites, he thought as he noted her reactions to the movie. She was so caught up in the movie, she didn't notice anything else.

Reed had grown up in a neighborhood where boys had to fight or be picked on, so he'd learned early on to fight and to pay attention to who was where, always.

He viewed her as he would a child, or any other innocent civilian, who hadn't learned to be wary. He was glad to see her relaxing and enjoying the movie.

This was why men like him fought. To protect the innocent, and preserve a peaceful way of life and freedom. These were some of the reasons he fought. Actor Cole Kennick played roles in which he did the same, which was one reason Reed enjoyed watching his movies.

Some feeling he couldn't have named, other than to call

it a sixth sense, made him turn his focus to a man dressed all in black.

Definitely not one of the staff.

Another patron, perhaps. He stood at the far right corner of the theater.

Something about him was very off.

The man turned to face the crowd, and began to move his arm upward —

Damn

Reed went calm and cool, even as he thought the word, his training kicking in, knowing the man was going to shoot.

Everything around Reed slowed.

"Everyone down!" he yelled, as his hand landed on the pretty blonde's shoulder, forcing her to the ground behind the seats.

The shooter raised his gun to fire.

SAMPLE CHAPTER: SAVING THE BELLYDANCER

2011

Little Creek, Virginia

Navy SEAL Antonius (Tony) "Cutter" Cuttino slid his six-foot frame behind the wheel of his red Corvette. Starting the car up and then shifting gears, he pulled the car out of the garage and down the driveway before backing into the street.

As he headed to Chicks Oyster Bar, he thought about his buddy's upcoming wedding.

Cutter getting married will change everything.

Change, however, was a part of life.

Chicks Oyster Bar, located at the Marina, was a big SEAL hangout. This was where the guys would throw the bachelor party. Many SEALs married bartenders or waitresses they'd met there, and women looking to meet a SEAL knew it was a possibility that one of the fit, handsome guys who frequented the bar was a SEAL.

Cutter had met his share of women at the bar, but none of those get togethers had lasted more than a month. He hadn't been looking for anything long term. He'd entered the Navy, wanting to see the world first, without having to worry about a family or a permanent girlfriend.

His grandmother was still living, and other than a large group of cousins, she was the only family he had in the states to come back to. His job as a SEAL suited his adventurous soul.

Still fit and mentally sharp, his grandmother had her circle of friends and stayed busy, though she was always happy to hear from Tony or be surprised by his visits.

Thinking of her, he reminded himself to call her tomorrow before the day was over.

Reed Tindall "Railroad" aka "R.T." would soon be getting married to Christie Anderson, a cute little floral designer who worked at Floral Blessings. R.T. had lucked out meeting Christie. With her blonde hair and curves, she looked like a gorgeous pin-up girl, and wearing 1940's style dresses and heels which was her big hobby. If Cutter had been as lucky as R.T., and met a woman like Christie, he might have considered a permanent relationship too. He wouldn't want her to get away.

Glad he hadn't met the woman of his dreams yet; he was happy for his friend.

After Becky, the girl who'd sent him a chickenshit Dear John letter, Cutter made sure none of the girls he dated lasted longer than a month. He had fun, he treated women right, but he wasn't about to get tied down. He made it clear that their fun was for a short time only. Anything else was a deal breaker. He wasn't about to get his heart broken again by another damn letter.

It was easier for a SEAL not to have a girl to worry about back home. There were women to be found in every port in the world. It wasn't as if he lacked female companionship. Being a SEAL, and a tall dark and handsome Italian American, he drew women like a magnet.

R.T. had been a carefree single man too, until meeting Christie. Then no other woman caught his eye. That was a sign, if anything were, that they were meant to be. But the couple had an unusual first meeting story.

They'd met at the movie premiere of the Cole Kennick movie Stand and Deliver when they'd sat next to each other. A live shooter had entered the building.

R.T. had taken out the shooter and then had to apply tourniquets to two men before they bled out.

He'd saved Christie's life, and then talked her through applying the second tourniquet to save the second man's life. The way she'd handled herself had him seeing a side to her that drew him in beyond her blonde bombshell looks. Afterward he'd seen her safely home. From that night on, they'd dated constantly, and she became the only woman Railroad was interested in.

Christie kept saying it was the worst and the best day of her life. While it wasn't R.T.'s worst, he never talked to her about the worst day of his life, he agreed with Christie that it was the best day of his life too.

Cutter had been with R.T. on the worst day of his life and had been one of the ones to save R.T. One of the team. They'd been on that mission together, and all come home together, which was nothing short of a miracle. It had knit them all tighter together than anything else would or could have and that bond of brotherhood was now unbreakable.

Each man would be celebrating this wedding with everything a SEAL had in him, because each knew how short and precious life could be. This meant it was going to be one hell of a party. For many reasons.

First was the theme. The bridal party would all be wearing 1940's style clothing.

Cutter looked forward to seeing the ladies dolled up and to swing dancing which sounded like fun. He'd never done any swing dancing, but Christie had arranged for an evening lesson for the whole wedding party.

Cutter was a quick learner, like most SEALs.

He'd have yet another skill to add to the ever-growing list of things he knew how to do. Watching his grandmother in her thirst for learning, he knew it was a lifestyle and a way of thinking that would keep him young. She seemed younger than her age, and her high spirits had a youthful way to them.

Tonight, he was meeting the guys at the bar and getting the scoop on what else was planned for the bachelor party they were all looking forward to. It would of course be at Chicks and involve shots, stories, and maybe a challenge or two.

Partnered with one of Christie's 1940's group friends, Cutter looked forward to dancing. He watched as the first couple, who taught the dances, demonstrated the dance they'd be learning. Swing dancing was well named. He watched the couple swing around the floor, the man swinging the smaller woman as if she weighed hardly a thing.

R.T. had a great big grin on his face as he looked at his fiancé. She wore a glow which was undeniable. Anyone viewing the scene could have picked out the bride to be as they both were clearly in love, and she wore that glow well-loved women often take on. R.T. couldn't keep his hands off her, something Cutter wasn't used to seeing. It made him grin. They were like a couple of teenagers.

Cutters dance partner was a dark-haired girl with blue eyes. He'd always been drawn to dancers, loved their legs and the way they moved, so normally his dance partner would've held his attention and interest, but their chemistry was off, and her high-pitched laugh grated on his nerves more than a little.

But when the music started, he set that aside and concentrated on learning the dance steps and moves so he could swing his partner around the room.

At the end of the hour, it hadn't been so bad. He'd kept her busy dancing not chatting, and the hour was up. It had been fun.

Though he'd be paired with whoever Christie desired in the wedding party, he wouldn't be escorting her as his date. He'd find a date. There was time. Too bad he couldn't be paired with Tanya, Christies best friend who was beautiful and fun to talk to. But she already had a boyfriend, so that was a no go.

It wasn't as if he had trouble getting dates. He'd find someone.

Local belly dancer "Zarifah" entered the dance studio late. She'd missed troupe rehearsal and was supposed to stay afterward to practice her veil solo where she could use the two walls of mirrors and the large space.

Her apartment was much too small to spin around in with a veil, without knocking things over, and she couldn't do that anymore. Not with the porcelain figurines Hassan had given her decorating the rooms.

The beautiful gifts were too expensive and treasured by her to risk them, so she no longer danced in her apartment, even without a veil. She missed dancing there.

Amina, the studio owner and troupe director, saw her coming through the door and said, "I wondered where you were," then she took a few steps toward her, a frown coming over her face as she took a closer look and saw bruises covering the left side of Zarifah's face. "Honey, what happened to you? Are you all right?"

"He came back. Last night." She spoke quiet, though there was no one else in the studio to hear her. It was still hard, sharing what had happened, even with one of her closest friends.

"Oh no. Honey, who did that to you?" Their eyes met and then Amina's eyes widened, as she realized who had done it. "Hassan."

"Yes." Zarifah nodded. "Luckily, my neighbor, Mrs. Dieter, called the police. Or I might not be here with you tonight. He was so very angry."

"Come in," Amina gently touched her elbow, to guide her in, and then pulled her hand back, as if afraid she might hurt her. "Was that okay? I don't want to touch you where it hurts."

"Yes. I'll be fine. I'm just a bit beat up at the moment." She gave a slight shrug.

Though this was a different kind of bruising, Zarifah had grown accustomed to bruises left by gymnastics when she was young and still learning. Her sights set on the Olympics, she and her coaches had pushed her hard back then.

Bruising happened. You got over it.

She set her jaw, summoning that determination which she'd learned at a young age training for the Olympics.

Amina pulled a chair around for her. "Sit. Rest. I will make us some tea. Then I want you to tell me what happened."

"Okay." Zarifah sat, but didn't relax in the chair. She hadn't relaxed since the night the man she'd thought she loved, who she thought had loved her, had turned into a monster. She wondered if she would ever relax again.

Amina loved tea and any excuse to make it. Tonight was

no exception. "Chamomile this evening, I think. It's a soothing tea. Sound good?"

Zarifah nodded and then watched her friend as she readied the small, portable tea maker, pouring water into it before starting the water to boil. Once the tea was ready, Amina would want her to tell everything that had happened with Hassan.

Hopefully the bruises will be gone before our next performance. If not, I'll have to bow out. Hassam will get his wish if I'm not dancing. I don't want anyone taking photos or video of me looking like this.

She had to tell Amina and she also needed to tell her that Hassan was dangerous, in case he ever showed up near any of the other dancers.

They were used to him and wouldn't see him as dangerous, so everyone needed to be told. It wouldn't be right to keep it private and keep them in the dark.

Security at the venues in their dance schedule wouldn't have seen him before. She'd run through the list of places in her head, on the drive over, to remember if he'd ever come to watch her dance at any of them. He hadn't.

She wished she hadn't burned all her pictures of him last night and blocked him on social media, when she'd been too upset to think she might need one photo of him. She'd been thinking she never wanted to see his face again.

They would have to find a picture of him somewhere, somehow. To give to security.

Maybe Amina can help.

It was important that all their dance sisters be safe.

Cutter was running late for the first half of the bachelor party at the Sweet Kitty Kat Club and didn't want to miss the main event. They would watch the girls and then move on to Chicks for drinking games and hot chicks.

Being on the SEAL teams meant you could be called away on short notice, for a good long time, and called away often. That made it hard on girlfriends, fiancés and wives. RT had worried that Christie might not be able to deal with the lifestyle. But she was sure she wanted this. Time would tell, but they had a good chance of making it last.

Christie was a good woman. R.T. had made a wise choice in her. She was a real cutie with her retro pinup outfits and good girl next-door good looks. The wedding party would be in n Navy dress uniforms for the men, and the women would be in vintage dresses like Marilyn Monroe would have worn. The kind that showed off their all curves. Cutter was all for that look and looking forward to all the eye candy at the wedding.

He couldn't have been happier for the couple. RT was happier than Cutter had ever seen him and Cutter could envision the two of them as a happily married gray haired couple in their twilight years together. He wanted that too, when he grew old.

But that was far into the future. He was living in the now, the today. Because that was all anyone ever really had.

Tonight, Cutter was running late to the party, but with any luck, the headline dancer wouldn't have started yet. He enjoyed watching dancers, with their long legs that could wrap around a man, and their toned bodies, which moved in ways that made him think of moving with them in a more intimate way across the sheets.

Dancers were hot. This first half of the party at the strip club should be good.

He sped up, his mind on long legged females stripping.

While he was glad for R.T., and their other buddy, SEAL Tanner "Diesel" Taylor who had a wife and two kids now, he wasn't ready to find his own wife and settle down. He was too busy having fun in between deployments. Dating strippers was part of that fun.

~

The next morning Tony's cell phone rang, vibration mode making it dance on the nightstand.

He reached for the phone. His eighty-year-old grandmother was calling, so he answered. "Good morning, grandma," he said as he glanced at the stripper sleeping next to him in his bed.

"So Tony, when are you going to come home and see your grandmamma?" his grandmother asked.

"Who's on the phone, baby?" Tawny asked. She ran her hand up his thigh. "Come here."

His grandmother kept on as if she hadn't heard the woman. "Nicki has three babies already and you never even married."

He turned away from Tawny, stood up and walked away, holding up a finger to her to wait. "Yes, Grandma, I know. Nicki has a new baby every year. I'm happy for her. She deserves the best."

Nicki was a neighborhood girl he'd dated in high school.

Tawny got out of bed, and started pulling her clothes on. He watched her naked body as she covered it with clothes, while he listened to his grandma.

Tawny had a great body. Long, sexy legs. Big breasts that bounced. She'd also gotten drunk last night after they got to his place and had been wild, as strippers often were. One thing he liked about them.

He rolled his left shoulder feeling the scratches she'd made across his back. Those long silver painted fingernails of hers were killer. He'd made her scream a few times. Noisy sex that could wake the neighbors.

He walked into the other room to be further away from her, as he talked to his grandmother, so he could pay better attention to his grandmother as she continued to talk.

"When you gonna get married, Tony. I want to be holding my own great grandbabies, not somebody else's," his grandmother said. "You gonna get yourself killed doing all that crazy stuff. I want you home soon. Marry. Have lots of babies."

He laughed. "Grandma, I'm not ready for marriage yet. The girl has to be the right girl, you know?"

"I know you're too picky," she said. "What one you have there with you this morning? Is she even Italian?"

Tawny was a hot blonde, with blue eyes, and was not the kind of girl he would bring home to meet his grandmother. *Definitely not Italian.* "Not Italian. I need to take her home, grandma. I'll call you later on today."

"Okay, Tony," she said. "But don't forget about your old grand-mamma."

"I would never forget about you, grandma. And you are not old. I'm planning to visit you soon. We can talk later."

"Okay, you go and take that one home. Then find one you can marry. I'm not getting any younger, you know."

"I love you grandma," he said.

"I love you too, Tony boy."

"Talk to you soon, grandma. Bye bye."

"Okay, bye bye." She hung up the phone and then he hung up.

She was only person he knew that he said, 'bye bye' to. After his parents had passed, his grandma was all the family he had.

An only child, it was up to him to carry on the family name and give his grandmother some grand-babies to fuss over. She was right; he did need to visit her. But not with a potential wife. He could fly home for a weekend and then fly back. He had plenty of leave and as she'd said, she wasn't getting any younger.

When he got back to Tawny, she'd crossed her arms and was giving him the stink eye expression. Why, he didn't know, as he'd thought the sex was good last night, for both of them.

"So your real name is Tony?" Tawny said. "Is there a reason you told me your name is Cutter, not Tony?"

"That is my name. They're both my names. Call me Cutter," he said.

"But your grandma calls you Tony," she said.

"That's right."

She took out a cigarette and lit it. Something she hadn't done last night. But he'd realized once they were naked in bed that she was a smoker. Because smoke wasn't just on her clothes from working in the club. Once she removed all her clothes and he began kissing her skin and her lips he could taste that she was a smoker.

He would never marry a woman who smoked. It was a real turn off for him. He regretted inviting her back to his place last night.

Maybe his grandmother was right, he needed to start dating a different kind of woman.

"I'm ready to go," she said. "You gonna buy me breakfast?"

"Sure." He reached for his keys. "Where do you want to go?"

"There's a waffle place around the corner from the club."

"Okay." He nodded. "Let's go." He'd feed Tawny, drop her off at her car, say goodbye, and then, make sure she drove away safely. But first, since he needed a date for the wedding, and he was out of time, he'd ask her if she'd like to go.

She seemed to have a thing for SEALs and had mentioned she'd dated a SEAL before. Then she'd peeled off her top, revealing those marvelous breasts and walked toward him. Watching them bounce he'd forgotten about her comment.

Now he wondered who the guy was.

"Here you go." Amina handed Zarifah a cup of hot tea. Sitting back in her chair, she put her full attention on Zarifah. "Now, tell me everything. From the beginning. I only knew that you had called off your engagement to Hassan."

"From the beginning." Zarifah took a deep breath. "Okay." She nodded. "The reason I called off our engagement," she frowned, paused, and then decided to start over.

Amina patiently waited for her to get on with the story.

"From the moment Hassan put the ring on my finger, everything changed," Zarifah said. "He changed. It was as if he was a different person."

"Oh no," Amina said.

"He did *not* want me dancing." Zarifah frowned.

"He didn't? I thought Hassan loved your dancing," Amina said. "He was always enthusiastic, usually clapping the loudest and he came to all our shows and was encouraging afterward." Amina's face showed her surprise.

Apparently, Hassan had fooled her too.

"Oh, he loves it all right. But only for him." Zarifah shook her head. "He said I would only dance in private for him from now on. And, from now on, meant, right this minute. Not after we got married, not after the shows I've already committed to."

"If you need to pull from a show, I will understand," Amina said. "It's okay. Just keep coming to the studio to dance with us. We would miss you terribly if you left."

"No, that's not what I need," Zarifah shook her head and frowned. "Hassan is unreasonable. *He* is the problem. He insisted I would not wear a belly dance costume outside of his house, or ever dance in public again, after we were engaged."

"Ah. His Middle Eastern upbringing is coming out." Amina nodded. "That's how he was raised. Wives don't dance, except in private at home, or with other women. Not even at weddings. The only dancers there are the hired belly dancers. He doesn't understand it's different here in the United States. These are cultural differences."

"Very true. He seemed more open minded when we were just dating. Never showed any signs of this kind of attitude before." Zarifah's forehead crinkled. "I had no idea he would change like he has. He couldn't seem to understand that I have commitments. That I'd agreed to do shows and I'm on troupe contract. I can't just drop everything, because he snaps his fingers and says right now." She shook her head. "And I can't marry a man who expects me to jump, just because he says jump."

"No, you can't." Amina shook her head along with Zarifah, agreeing with her. "Wives are partners, not trained dogs."

Zarifah continued with her story, telling it for the first time, to a good friend. "So I knew I couldn't marry him. That was the conclusion I came to, about us, and I told him the next night, after he still wouldn't see reason and change his mind about my dancing. When there was no talking it out, I said, 'I can't do this any more. You won't listen to me or discuss this reasonably. I can't marry you.' I called the engagement off."

"Well, you had no other choice. It's a good thing you called it off before you were married," Amina said.

Zarifah remembered how she'd held out the ring to Hassan, to give it back, but he hadn't taken it. He wouldn't even look at the ring.

"I took the ring off to hand it to him, but he wouldn't take it," she said.

"Oh no." Amina's tone held dread for what was likely coming next in Zarifah's tale.

"He said, 'You're just nervous. It will pass. Brides get nervous. You are my betrothed. My perfect jewel. I have been searching for you for years, and now that I have found you, I will never let you go'," Zarifah said.

Amina's eyes widened. "Never let you go. Oh that does *not* sound good. Not when you are calling things off and *want* him to let you go."

"I was in shock. Speechless. I just stood there with my hand out," Zarifah paused, shaking her head. "He ignored my hand, the ring, my shocked expression, and he acted as if everything was normal. Then he kissed my cheek goodbye, told me to get some sleep, that I'd feel better in the morning and he was out the door before I could even think what to do next."

"Wow." Amina sat back in her chair, as if she too was shocked.

"It was as if he didn't see me or hear me beyond the role he wants me to be in. I didn't know what to do. He hurried out the door and I was sort of stunned."

"Sort of? That would shake any woman. Especially after pulling a Jekyll and Hyde switch you weren't prepared for. Of course he took you by surprise."

"Maybe he's never seen me. I mean really seen me." Zarifah shook her head. "Maybe he never saw past the dancer to see the real me."

"I think you are right," Amina said. "He sounds like one of those who wants the dream, not the real woman. He sees Zarifah, the dancer, his beautiful dream girl. Not Edith, the woman behind that image."

This was true.

Zarifah was her dance name. Dance was only a part of who she was. But it was a part that she loved, and which brought her joy.

He saw no problem with her dropping everything and just walking away.

She would never do that. Besides being their troupe director, Amina was her friend. The other dancers were her friends. But even if they hadn't been, she wouldn't go back on her promises and her commitments. She wasn't that kind of person.

This major problem between them, which had made her step back to take a closer look at him and where things were headed, had changed her mind completely about marrying him.

She was an American belly dancer, with American sensibilities, living in the United States of America. Freedom was on an upper rung of the ladder of importance in her life. She could never marry a man who thought he could order her about, as if he owned her.

"Did he want you to give up teaching gymnastics too?" Amina asked. "Or just dance?"

"He didn't pay much attention to me teaching gymnastics," Zarifah said.

"No? But that's your job and also very much a part of you."

"True." Zarifah nodded.

It was very much a part of her, more than her dance persona.

Edith Smith was her real name, and the one everyone

associated with gymnastics. Trained from a young age, she had competed with an eye on Olympic gold, until she began to sprout up, taller than the other girls her age, her arms and legs growing so fast and awkward in just one summer.

The tallest girl in her elementary school class, Edith felt gangly and awkward, not graceful. She would grow tall and be more suited to basketball, than gymnastics. That's what her coaches had told her, as they'd turned their attention to younger, shorter girls, while dashing cold water on her dreams.

Now she taught gymnastics to children and was much kinder to them than her coaches had ever been to her.

Belly dancing was a fun hobby on the side.

Belly dancing was freedom.

Dancing, she competed with no one, while her gymnastics background gave her a unique style of dance, as the other dancers were not as flexible as she.

"It sounds as if you really didn't know him either," Amina said. "He didn't show you his true colors until now. And he didn't want to know the real you. Marriage to him would've been a major disaster."

"Yes, it would have," Zarifah agreed.

Dancing was where she felt most free. And she would never have given it up for Hassan.

She'd kept her dancing separate, using her dance name in public, and few people connected the two sides of her life, unless they were close enough to her for her to tell them.

Hassan had fallen for the dancer side. He'd been completely uninterested in the other side. He'd never seen her at work, never wanted to hear about it. She taught small children, that's all he cared to know. All he'd said after he'd asked her what she did for a living was, "Good. That means you will be a good mother, when you have children of your own."

They hadn't discussed whether she wanted to have children or not. She wouldn't mind having one or two, but it certainly wasn't what drove her. She had a career and a hobby and both took large chunks of her time. She'd been too focused on building her business to even think about having children of her own and she loved what she did.

The driven, competitive, athletic side of a woman who'd nearly gone to the Olympics as a child, that strong, female businesswoman wasn't what Hassan wanted. He wanted a woman he could control.

Zarifah could not be anything but what she was. Nor did she want to. She was very much a gymnast and she loved to dance with her troupe. If he couldn't love her, for who she was, she knew she had to call the engagement off.

Amina had been silent, listening, but now she spoke again. "So he walked out, leaving you holding that beautiful one-karat diamond ring with two rubies. Then what happened?"

"I overnighted the ring to him the next day, so he'd have to sign for it and accept it."

"Good. Smart lady." Amina nodded.

"I couldn't keep it. I don't want anything he gave me. But listen to this," she pulled her cell phone out of her bag and hit play.

Hassan's angry voice message played. "Zarifah, you do not throw my gifts back in my face with your messenger. You do not send your messenger to me, making me sign. I do not accept this. We are still engaged. You do not treat me like this!" His voice rose with each sentence as he became angrier.

"Oh no!" Amina had a horrified look on her face.

"He kept calling my phone, but I started deleting his

messages after this one and didn't listen to any more of them. Then it got real quiet and I thought he was done." She took a sip of tea and swallowed, for her throat had gone dry with what she had to tell next.

Amina said, "Oh no," and patiently waited for Zarifah to go on.

Zarifah took a deep breath and continued. "He showed up at my apartment and somehow got in. There's no sign of breaking and entering and I could've sworn I locked the door. I *always* lock the door. But he came in, some way. He had the ring and insisted I put it back on." She paused, frowning, remembering.

"Did you put it on?" Amina asked.

ACKNOWLEDGMENTS

My infinite love and gratitude to all who played a part in the origins of this story, all the way to this new launch of the revised story, and my new Green Brotherhood: SEAL Team XII series.

From the beginnings of the original short novella I was invited to write by Susan Stoker, and for recent encouragement to publish this story with my own press, my eternal thanks to Susan Stoker; Special thanks to Elle James who introduced me to Susan, and suggested I write in her world. Kindle Worlds was a good run while it lasted, and I appreciate you both inviting me into your worlds.

Thank you to my gun instructor and gunfight scene advisor for many years, Army veteran Bobby Buls; thank you to Marine veteran and advisor Charles Welshans; thank you to Delilah Devlin for editing several of my books in the series; thank you to my cover artist Sheri L. McGathy; and to my sister Kim who read all my books and worked as my PA; thank you to my best friend author Susan Boles; and to all my readers who loved that first short story and wanted more.

From that first small novella, grew this new series I'm excited to launch with this first book, and I'm thrilled to be able to thank my new SEAL advisor, Navy SEAL veteran and author Bill Hellman who is helping me make my SEAL stories even better and worked with me to create this new SEAL Team; thank you to my cover artist and logo designer for SEAL Team XII Sheri L. McGathy; thank you to my family, and especially my husband Mike, bus driver, mainte-nance man, and sometimes "arm candy."

I love you all.

ABOUT THE AUTHOR

Debra Parmley is an adventurous, multi-genre author who lives in a motorhome full-time, with her husband, as they travel the U.S.A.

An Air Force veteran's wife, Debra writes military romantic suspense. She also writes contemporary romance, holiday romance, fairytale romance, 1920's romance, gritty western historical romance, futuristic romance, and time travel romance.

Debra says "Every day we are alive is a beautiful day," and she likes to give her readers and her story people a story that ends happily.

Her first romance, A Desperate Journey, a gritty western historical, was published in 2008 in eBook, and 2009 in print, after being selected as one of the novels to compete in the American Title II contest put on by Dorchester Publishing, and Romantic Times Book Lovers magazine. One year later, her agent sold the book in a traditional deal to a small press.

Debra has sold travel, walked the plank of a pirate ship, off the coast of Grand Cayman, swum with dolphins in Moorea in French Polynesia, escorted a bus full of people through Scotland, and set foot in over 13 countries.

She married her high school sweetheart, whom she asked out on a five-dollar bet. After living in several states with her husband and two sons, and then living for 23 years just outside Memphis, TN, in Bartlett, she and her husband sold their home and moved into a 43-foot motorhome, a Tin Allegro bus, where they live full-time.

In the summer of 2022, they lived and worked on a sandbar, in Rodanthe, on Hatteras Island, in the outer banks of North Carolina. In early 2023, they worked as gate guards, guarding oil rigs in Texas. Their current adventure is living and working for six months in Cody, Wyoming, the rodeo capitol of the world. Then they will be off on their next adventure.

Debra writes about their travels and is working on a book about their first year on the read.

For more about her travels, visit her Beautiful Day Traveler blog or her YouTube Channel.

As Debra Bishop, she writes fairy tales for all ages, fantasy, and children's books.

www.debraparmley.com

ALSO BY DEBRA PARMLEY

ROMANTIC SUSPENSE:

Military Romantic Suspense:

Green Brotherhood SEAL Team XII:

Finding Bryce, book one - eBook, paperback

Real Movie Hero, book two – eBook, paperback

Saving the Bellydancer, book three – eBook, paperback

Brotherhood Protectors series:

Montana Marine - eBook, paperback

Defensive Instructor - eBook, paperback

Marine Protector - eBook, paperback

Blind Trust - eBook, paperback

A Triple C Ranch Christmas Wedding - eBook, paperback

Montana Delta Rescue - eBook, paperback

Montana SEAL Protector - eBook, paperback

White Horse Wedding – eBook, paperback - 2023

Montana Rodeo Protector - eBook, paperback – 2023

Romantic Suspense:

Bobbins Sisters Trilogy:

Check Out – book one, eBook, paperback, audiobook

Check In – book two, eBook, paperback

Check Up – book three, 2023

Single Title:

Aboard the Wishing Star - eBook, paperback, audiobook

Jenna's Christmas Wish - eBook, paperback

To Catch an Elf – 2023

HISTORICAL ROMANCE:

Western Historical Romance:

Gone to Texas: A Desperate Journey - (original, sweeter version) - Large Print Hardcover, eBook, paperback

Dangerous Ties - eBook, paperback, audiobook

Deadly Adversaries - eBook, paperback

Desperate, Dangerous, Deadly: A Western Collection – eBook

Isabella, Bride of Ohio: American Mail Order Bride – (sweeter version) - Large Print Hardcover, eBook, paperback

Penny From Deadwood – eBook, paperback 2023

1920's Romance:

Trapping the Butterfly – book one, eBook, paperback, audiobook, Large Print Hardcover

Dancing Butterfly – book two, eBook, paperback

Exotic Butterfly – book three, 2024

FAIRY TALE AND FANTASY ROMANCE:

The Twelve Stitches of Christmas – (short story) – eBook

Vague Directions - eBook, paperback- 2023

FUTURISTIC DYSTOPIAN ROMANCE

The Hunger Roads Trilogy:

Another Change of Scenery – 2023

Down a Back Road – 2023

Into the Convergence Zone – 2024

POETRY

Poetry Anthology:

Twilight Dips – eBook, print

NONFICTION:

Travel Memoir:

Anywhere But Here: Our First Year Living on the Road - 2023

OUT OF PRINT:

Protecting Pippa

Split Screen Scream

Protecting Zarifah

Vague Directions – short story

A Desperate Journey

Isabella, Bride of Ohio

Tales From Deadwood - anthology

We Know the Truth, Do You? Area 51 – anthology (going to the moon/time capsule)

Wounded Heroes - anthology

Hansel & Gretel: Down the Rabbit Hole – anthology

More Monsters from Memphis – anthology